SIN:THETICA

"...readers are treated to a thought-provoking exploration of what it means to be human in an increasingly digital world, led by a flawed yet determined protagonist whose journey is as much one of self-discovery as it is a quest for justice. Baird delivers a satisfying blend of thrills, mystery, bloodbaths, and philosophical depth."
—Booklife Review from Publishers Weekly

"A first-person bounty hunter romp under the neon lights of cyberpunk purgatory. In Hendrix, Baird has created a main character who combines the unrelenting violence and one-liners of Judge Dredd, Blade, and The Punisher. Hendrix is then thrown into a science fiction fever dream where the stakes are high and nothing is as it seems."
—Adam Hulse, author of *Below Economic Thresholds*

"I'll be very honest here, this genre is not one I've read previously, but Baird's imagination, way with words, and excellent characterization plugged me into *SIN:THETICA* rather quickly. I loved following the main character Balaam Hendrix around futuristic NeuTokyo with his snappy dialogue, no-nonsense demeanor, and remaining humanity underneath his rugged exterior. You root for him even when he's doing something seemingly awful. One minute you think you know what's happening and then, well, you don't. Give this novella a read and tell me you aren't instantly pulled into Baird's futuristic world; one you might not even realize you're in as you're twisting and turning in your own Grav."
—Vivian Kasley, horror writer published in *Hot Iron and Cold Blood*, *Crimson Bones*, and other anthologies

SIN:THETICA

by Keith Anthony Baird

SIN:THETICA

Edited by S.D. Vassallo

Formatted by Stephanie Ellis

Cover illustration and design by Alexander Way-B

First Edition: May 2024

ISBN (paperback): 978-1-957537-99-3
ISBN (ebook): 978-1-957537-98-6
Library of Congress Control Number: 2024935808

BRIGIDS GATE PRESS

Overland Park, Kansas

www.brigidsgatepress.com

Printed in the United States of America

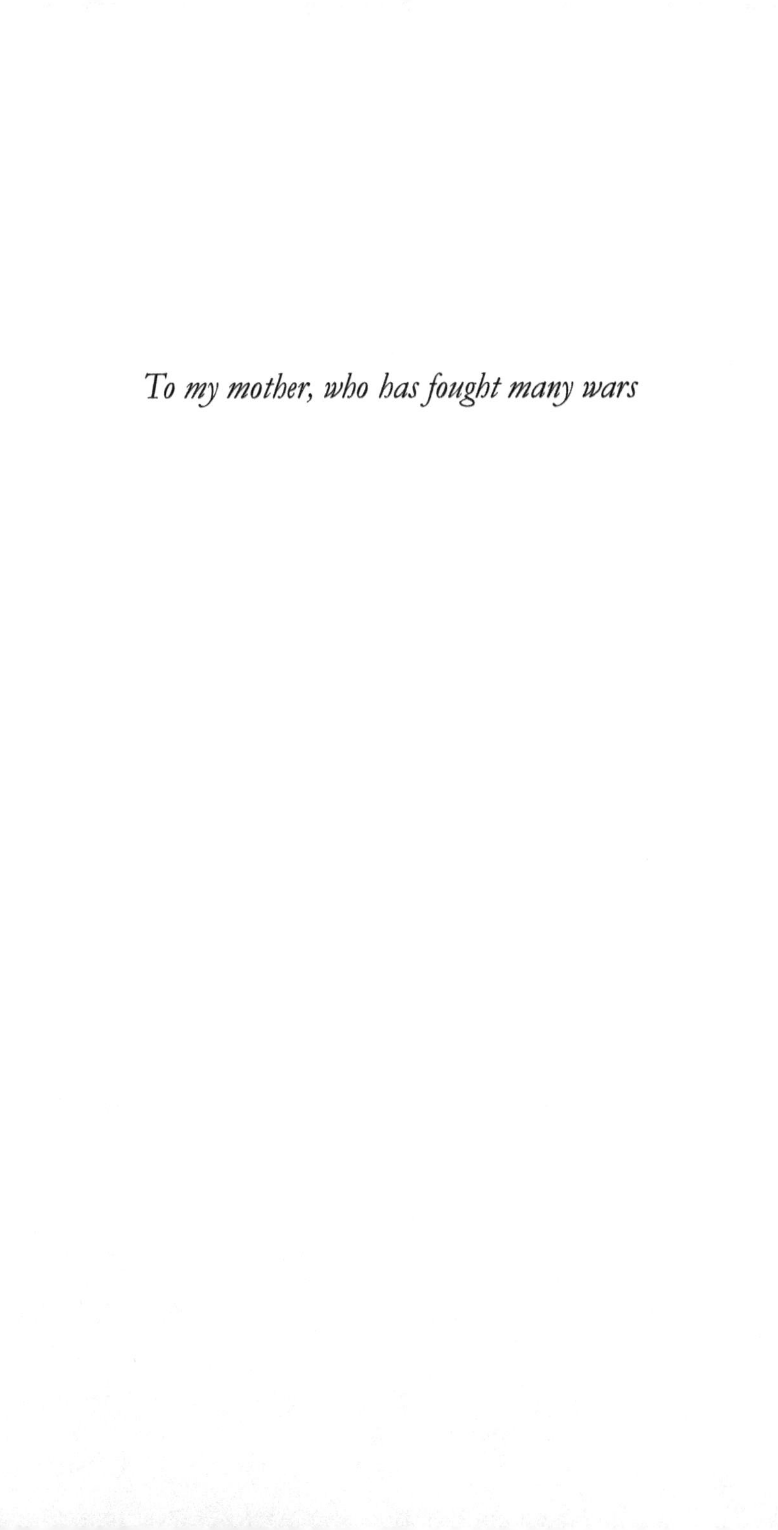

To my mother, who has fought many wars

Content warnings are provided at the end of this book

Just So You Know ...

The first time I saw NeuTokyo was when I arrived on a dropship in my Coalition Marine Corps unit. We hit the bay in the last exchanges of the Sino-Nippon War in '97. I remember how it seemed a lure of photo-neon and high-rise clusters, set against shimmering water filled with isobunes, junks, and delta freighters. It's an image which stayed with me and part of the reason I never left. Our emblem, the Cowl of the Shaolin Cobra, was laid low in the days after as we suffered the worst losses of the campaign. As our front line advanced beyond the fallen city, we were cut to pieces by the enemy's guerrilla tactics in the suburbs. All I recall was the moment our carrier was hit by a particle round and the pulse which snapped its chassis like a toothpick.

I have no recollection of the hail of bullets they put into me, after I was thrown clear of the wreck. Had I not coughed up blood inside that body bag, they never would have spent months putting me back together.

But the military ditched what was no longer of any use to them and the city became my new home. It was tough at first. Nothing short of a combat crawl through yet more hostile terrain, and for me, mostly devoid of meaning. Then out of that chaos Antoyah entered my life. Quiet, serene Antoyah. We married, and not long after, our child was born. Life was good. I was complete.

Those were days of peace and tranquillity, love, and laughter. Rehabilitated from my injuries I found paydays in security work, mostly guarding shipments or so-called VIPs. They were assholes in the main but the jobs paid handsomely enough, granting my family a comfortable existence in a decent neighbourhood. We thrived for a time, in all the ways that can make life rich and full of meaning until NeuTokyo's crime rate began to spiral, putting the district on a downward trajectory.

Fearing a spread of the problem the authorities put a ban on any relocation efforts. What it did was put good folk at the mercy of organised crime. In time, the hood was branded a favela: drug-lord-ruled territory. And though a civilian, it felt like I was back on the battlefield, and once again, in someone else's war. After sundown was the worst of it. The nightly body count and the eerie calm the day after. I feared for my wife and child.

Then of course, inevitable given the hellscape our daily routine had become, there came that dreaded knock at the door. That night, the lords of the favela came and took my life away. I've often wondered why. Pondered the reason but I always come full circle. It was nothing short of simply taking what I had. My wealth. My soulmate. My flesh and blood. I had to watch as they set fire to our home, and with it, my wife and child. I had to endure their awful end before a knuckleduster blow put me under.

It's now 2113, over a decade and a half later, and I hunt people for a living in this lawless place. On the fractious border, justice is whatever you want it to be and those with enough wealth make it so. They call me The Reverend, and if I'm paid to find you, then it's a given I'll be giving you your Last Rites.

Damage Incorporated

The rain brings a certain silver on black when the dark hours lend their arc to the city. It's easy to lose yourself in the glimmer of a downpour. Will it wash away everything that's wrong here, or will it just bring more of the same? I've heard it said NeuTokyo storms are the most violent in the Asia-Pacific, but I doubt that's true. That said, they do lash away like something wild, and leave your heart colder in the aftermath. The sky's purging right now as I step into this door recess and use its depth for cover. The shadows swallow me and I've now got eyes on the Grav-Mechanica parked across the broadway. The air blast from the Bullet-Tram which roars past almost makes my Dakota hat airborne. My hideout is illuminated and I stand out like a dog's balls. Then it passes and it's dark again. I pull my overcoat collar up and take a long drag on my No-Glo cigar.

Four days of gathering intel has led me to this shithole and I'm not about to give another hour to this payday. Time is money and so it ends right here, tonight. Ganz, Emanuel J, has been sucking on limited air for a while now, but the clock's all out of kindness and his days as part of the Soul Syndicate are done. He'll be leaking fast on the streets of the Kabukicho District and I'll be downing Pacific Port rum for what's left of the post meridiem. Taking the safety off my Magnum-Drive pistol, I drop it back into its hip holster and swear because I'm getting cold out here.

"Don't keep me waiting, you miserable fuck."

I'm answered shortly by the splice of light and pulse of music which spills from the brothel's side door, before it slams shut just as fast. Ganz has just stepped out, and I watch the intermittent flare of his vapourtube as he makes his way towards the vehicle. The rain's easing now, from a drench to a steady soak. I join the crowd on the street, walking parallel to my mark. I keep my head down, not looking in his direction. I'm like any other Joe making his way home through the storm.

Yet the greaseball still makes me. Got a sixth sense or something. Remotely activating the gull-wing door, he hauls up about six feet in front of it. Lowering his cooling vapourtube, he turns and looks me dead in the eye.

We're about thirty feet apart, with a lot of traffic between us. Maybe he figures I can't make the shot. Or, if I do, I'll just hit a random passerby. What he doesn't know is I don't give a fuck. I'd rather just send him to Hell, but if some Johnny Innocent gets in the way, it won't keep me up at night. And it won't save his life. The rounds I use will go through anyone in the way and punch my mark's ticket too. So I stand there, holding his gaze, waiting for him to react.

I've been in hundreds of face-offs, and I guess one day I'll be on the wrong side of the age game, and I'll have lost my edge. But that's not today, and Ganz is about to wear the toe tag of kill number ninety-four. The tram has finished its red-light district circular, and I can see it hurtling its way back out of the corner of my eye. I've got about five seconds before it's going to cut off the gap between me and my quarry. It'll hand Ganz an exit route if I don't act now. And I know he's noticed it too, as a 'fuck you' grin starts to etch across that smarmy face of his. It's nothing but pure reflex these days, but I've already drawn and dropped the hammer on the single shot I'm firing.

The crack of the discharge is lost in the howl of the approaching transporter but he clocks the muzzle flare. Skill, lucky timing, and a sense of the uncanny converge to make what will be the city's most talked about takedown. I see everything in slow motion for an instant before it all ends again in real time. In that stitch in time the bullet glides through the random steps of countless city crawlers, whizzing millimetres from some and inches from others. It shatters the window of a speeding retro taxi cab and exits its passenger side counterpart. Unchecked in its flight path, it connects again with a passing automated Garbage Grav for some interesting 'sideways' consequences.

Essentially of steel and rubber makeup, the Grav is equipped with a whole host of robotic limbs and tools rigged for waste collection. Struck by the bullet and sheared clean off, the rear-mounted foot-long hydraulic pincers are sent spinning through the air to the far side of the broadway. The Bullet Tram roars past, cutting off my view and I wait for the 8:15 Shinjuku Looper to clear the vicinity. Through the ever distant clatter of its monorail track I pace towards my mark. His car is still parked outside the Grinding Hydra whorehouse, door ajar, drivetrain on standby, but missing its driver.

Hell, it was always going to be that way. There was no way Ganz was stepping off that sidewalk and evading my intent. I look down and scan the litter the city's automated collector didn't get to pick up. There's Ganz's vapourtube, now cooling fast in the rain. There's the telltale blood, merging with the gutter pools. And here's the crowd of onlookers who've stopped to gasp at the sight of a bounty hunter's day at the office.

I follow their stares and find my prize—a gift, courtesy of a rogue municipal garbage tool. I pick it up, duck into an alleyway, and it isn't long before I'm approaching my own parked-up car. I remote-open the doors just as Ganz did, and when I reach it I throw my evidence inside by its long, lank hair. His head nestles sweetly into the contour of the passenger seat and I tell my Grav to fire up before I step in. You can't get a payday without any proof and Ganz's face isn't looking quite so smug anymore.

***

The surgeon that patched me up didn't care all that much. To him, I was a nobody. He used an organic weld on my left shoulder, then stitched me back up. Sloppy work. I can feel things moving around, and grating against each other. I've learned to accept the pain, and when it gets bad, some rum and a Narcoplex pill dulls the pain enough for me to function. Those little black pearls are my only true friends in this sprawl. I pop one and start to drift off, right as my proximity alarm goes off.

'Warning: Unknown male approaching. Counter measures primed and awaiting instruction.'

I don't get visitors. What's this fucking shit? The door monitor flares into life. I sit up on the bed and look at who's about to press the intercom button. Never seen this suit before. He looks a rat. The kind who'd sell his kids for a hike up the food chain. I smell money, but in a rotten way, which doesn't sit well with me. Gun in hand, I get up and slowly walk to the hall and keep a watch on the front door. The buzzer's already sounded twice but I'll wait for him to leave a recorded message. He's hovering … and now focuses on the pinhole camera in the door. It's a knowing smile which says 'I know you're there, so I'm not going to give you the satisfaction of leaving a bullshit message.' There's a surety to his posture I don't like, but I'll have to get face-to-face to size him up properly. He's about six steps back down the outer corridor when I open up and demand an explanation.

"Who the fuck are you? How did you find me?"

He floats back and assumes a false, friendly demeanour.

"You can put the gun away, Hendrix. I'm unarmed and here with a genuine offer from Arlen Vargas which could prove very lucrative for a man of your standing in the city."

There it is … the way he says that last bit like he already has me one click above dog shit.

"A man of my standing? Say something witty again and I'll be the only one standing."

He grins, rubs his chin, and looks at the floor. It's that telltale sign of self-belief and defiance, but I think he's wise enough to know I mean it.

"On any other day," he says, locking my gaze and wrestling with a desire to come at me.

Everything about him screams 'professional'—personal security, assassin, or something of that ilk. Whatever the case, he can see my manner has 'give me a fucking reason' painted all over it. With a quick smile it's all done, and he shifts from hard-ass mode back to the errand boy antics he's been handed.

"Listen, Hendrix, Mr. Vargas is a very powerful man and when he wants something he gets it. He's picked you to do a job for him and you're to be back in touch by the end of the day with the answer he's expecting to hear."

"You haven't answered my questions."

He rolls his eyes, sets his jaw, then answers. "Who I am is unimportant. Let's just say I'm an associate of Mr. Vargas. As for how I found you … finding people is just one of my particular talents."

"What if I don't want to be found? What then?"

"That's really not the point, Hendrix. Point is, your services are required and Mr. Vargas isn't the kind of man you want to fuck with."

I'm giving him my best 'so fucking what' look. "My ID is on the Spectre Grid. That's how all my jobs come in. Have your Mr. Vargas message me and I'll give it some thought."

"You're already being messaged. Off-Grid. And, I just told you … he's not a man to be fucked with."

Normally, I would've just dusted this cockroach by now, but Vargas is a heavy hitter on NeuTokyo's unspoken lethal bastard list and so I'm not going to shit in my own nest.

"I've got a rule. Whenever I do business, I talk to the organ grinder … not the monkey. You tell Vargas if he wants an answer by the end of the day, he'll have to contact me personally. Now take your rat-fuck face away from my door and put it back in his ass."

I don't even give him time to react as I hit the close pad on the door system and the hydraulics slam it shut.

***

It's been three days since I got my payout for Ganz and it's been around four hours since monkey boy showed up, and right when I'm thinking of knocking back the odd glass or three, an alert pops up on the Spectre Grid. I guess Vargas really does mean business. I use the auto-link to access the grid and ask who's there.

"Good evening, Mr. Hendrix. You insisted I call in person, so here I am."

"You plan on sending more meatheads my way?"

"That's funny language, Mr. Hendrix, but I assure you that won't be the case."

Vargas isn't the type to take orders from anyone, so he must really be in a jam. I expand the holographic link to get a visual. He's a thin man and not what I was expecting. His dark hair is slicked back and his pallor makes him look a little sickly in truth. Of course, his threads are worth more than my entire fortune and the odd piece of jewellery merely accentuates the net worth. There's that reptilian look that just about everyone who hires me has about them. The kind that lets you know they're capable of eating their babies, should it come to that.

I gesture for him to continue and he takes his time, but not in a defiant way. I've heard plenty of Vargas stories, and one that springs to mind right now is the Näder case. Apparently, he put his spacious pad on the market years ago before moving to where he currently resides. A sales agent turned up to conduct a valuation, and Vargas led the woman around the property. As urban legend goes, he continued nonchalantly through the dining room as the woman looked on in horror. The night before he'd invited business associates over for dinner, and if the rumours are to be believed, he had them decapitated midway through dessert. The bodies were still sat at the table the morning after.

I'm inclined to believe it.

"Mr. Hendrix, if you will allow me an indulgence, I'd like to take a moment to refresh my memory on one or two details before we go on."

I give a slight nod, like this is boring, and he continues. A sidekick pulls up a holo-page from the Spectre Grid, and Vargas casts his eye over it. He mutters a few things, and I catch "decorated war hero," "ex-Coalition Corps veteran," and "all-round indestructible son-of-a-bitch." He collapses the feed and chuckles a tad.

"You gave my associate the right answer earlier today, Mr. Hendrix. Had you bowed down to my request I'd have thought you a lesser man. And, for what I need you to do, you simply can't be any such thing."

I just stare at him blankly. Not because I'm trying to come across like I don't give a fuck. It's 'because' I don't give a fuck. He smiles, and continues.

"I like you, Mr. Hendrix. I believe our agendas are quite similar."

If he's looking for some kind of acknowledgement to that he's getting none. He raises an eyebrow and seems to ponder something.

"How many men have you killed?"

I give it a second's thought and answer. "I'm afraid your intel is quite off, Mr. Vargas. I only kill the elderly, the disabled, and juicy little infants."

He flat out laughs. "Oh, Mr. Hendrix, I do appreciate your wit."

I look around for that bottle I was going to get started on before he interrupted my day, and I answer as I find a glass and pour myself a measure.

"Well, you did just point out we're quite similar, Mr. Vargas."

The grin's dropped off his face and he's processing the insult as I take my first gulp of the spirit.

"That wasn't very hospitable, Mr. Hendrix. Let me be clear, I'll kill anyone that gets in my way. There's no room for sentiment in business. And speaking of business, let's get down to it."

"I've been waiting for that from the moment you buzzed on the grid."

He takes a quick intake of breath to steady his irritation and then gets on with it. "Three weeks ago, an employee went rogue and stole something of great value to me. Now, despite what you might think, I'm not a materialistic man, Mr. Hendrix. No, for me, it's the fact I gave him a living. I find that disrespectful and therefore I'd like you to find him, recover my property, and keep him intact for a demise of my choosing."

I knock back the remainder of the rum and decide to take a seat as I'm sick of standing now. I feel the need for a smoke coming on and so I light up a cigar and think about what he's just said. "You say three weeks ago. I assume your goons have spent that amount of time trying to find this guy and drawn a blank. Hence, why you're contacting me?"

He nods slightly and I can't help but make a comment I should probably leave well alone.

"Seems your staff are either disloyal or incompetent, Mr. Vargas. And you, being a man who likes concise action, no less."

It's obvious I've put my big fucking stick into the hornet's nest, as he's clearly riled by my remark. There's an ugly little snarl trying to form at the corner of his mouth and he takes a lingering look at anything but me.

"It's crass to relish in someone else's misfortune, Mr. Hendrix. I hope we're not getting off on the wrong foot here?"

I don't give him any clue I'm enjoying it, but I am, and he's undoubtedly smart enough to know that. Instead, I move the conversation right along. "We're good, Vargas. Give me the rest."

He takes a moment to focus, and then spills it. "I'm afraid I can't give you much to go on. Those in my organisation are ghosts, therefore I can't give you any standard matter you might use to track him down. Fingerprints are removed, and there's no retina scan on file anywhere. I can't even provide a DNA profile but what I can do is transfer a mug shot to your grid account. Of course, I will include everything else I know about him."

I ponder some of the angles of all that. "What if he's simply boarded a pirate freighter to anywhere but here?"

"Indeed, but all our tracking indicates he's not left the city. Let's just say I have connections in Zone Control and there's no data from them which shows otherwise."

What he's really saying is he's got dirt on middle management fucks at City Security. Whenever he needs to know someone's movements he'll use that leverage to acquire the information. I know how it works.

"So if he's not skipped town, why couldn't your goons find him given everything you know about his background?"

"That's the mystery, Mr. Hendrix, and that's exactly why I'm in need of your help."

"You got enemies who'd give him shelter?"

"Too many to mention."

"How much does he know about your setup which might leave you vulnerable?"

"What he knows doesn't concern me. What's important is to get my property back, and for him to get his hand slapped - to a pulp. If I don't punish him, then others will think they can get away with defiance too."

"I put my targets on the mortuary slab. You're wanting a living, breathing fuck-up returned to you. It's not what I do."

"Yes, Mr. Hendrix, I'm aware of that, which is why I'm tripling your normal fee."

He slowly leans forward, cocks his head slightly to one side, and delivers the final question through a jackal-like grin.

"Well, Mr. Hendrix, what shall it be? What shall it be?"

My gut's telling me to walk away from this poisoned chalice he's offering, but the money's always the lure. There'll come a day when I can't do this anymore, and I have to plan for that. Right now I'm torn and he's wanting an answer.

***

It's quite hypnotic how the shadows move within the districts when you're watching a NeuTokyo sunrise. The traffic's already building up out there and the lush amber-and-blood cocktail of colour is laced with all manner of Gravs. There are the private hires, the public shuttles, the Aeroquads with their design nod to historic motorcycles, and all makes and models of Mechanicas, from rust buckets to top-of-the-line examples.

My own sits on the aero-pad just beneath the window. It's a Chrysler Fury with black market modifications I've paid a handsome figure for. It's fast. And with the toys it's got, it don't get outclassed. Makes my job a whole lot easier. And, sadly … I see it's decorated with seagull shit again. I swear those fucks get everywhere.

I've got a 7:30 meeting with my arms dealer and I want to grab a caffeine bomb on the way, and maybe a bite to eat, from one of the street vendors. I'm rarely hungry when I first get up. I'll see if something whets my appetite. As I step out onto the aero-pad, the pulse of the city resonates against the apartment block, and I carry my hat instead of putting it on and having to fight the updraft. The gulls squawk at me and one gets a boot for the collective crap on my car.

They scatter to flight and I take a moment to grab the hosepipe nozzle hanging in its cradle, and then proceed to blast last night's meal off my windscreen. Inside and airborne, it's a five-minute flight to the central market and I've got a handful of time to kill before hooking up with Zheng Zhu. The traffic is its usual chaotic ballet of high-speed metal, with everyone adopting their 'fuck-off' mentality. How it's not a collision carnival is beyond me.

It's always struck me as odd how the photo-neon everywhere is left to run 24/7. Sure, it's a low power consumer, but it has to rack up year in, year out. Personally, I think it's looked upon as a permanent cosmetic for a place which would look a giant prison without it. I take a few quieter alleyways I know to help keep a cooler head in the mayhem. One time I saw a guy parking his Grav on his aero-pad, only to have some out-of-control asshole shunt him from behind and send the car crashing through his apartment wall. I mean, it's good having easy access to your home, but that's a bit too literal. It's always been this way here though. When I first got dumped into the culture when my Corps days were done, the city seemed a space I'd never get to grips with. But somehow it all seemed to fall into place and I found myself adjusting real quick. The backwater lifestyle of Liberty, Kentucky, never prepared me for the mega cities of my own country, never mind NeuTokyo.

When I first joined the International Coalition Corps I never thought I'd end up fighting for China in its offensive to acquire Japanese territory. But hell, that was the twenty-first century, a pretty fucked-up era. I guess I'm an adopted Sino now, but it doesn't much matter what I am. When the city fell a strange kind of transformation accompanied the takeover. From what I know it'd always been a melting pot of cultures, but after the '97 ceasefire the void was filled with Americans, Germans, the French, and Chinese.

Since then, there's been a whole host of migrants from all over who've repopulated the city. Always struck me as odd why the Chinese didn't just erase the Tokyo name tag, but I found out from Zheng the ruling party wanted the world to remember the jewel of Japan had been crushed. Hence, they simply added the 'Neu'—a symbol of their might on the world stage.

I settle on some crispy minute-noodles and spicy ripped chicken to put in the old organic fuel tank. Done, I put the litter in a trash can and take a sip of my tea as I head away from the food courts to rendezvous with my supplier. I'm low on ammunition, and I could do with some new tech for my home security system. Zheng's always got the latest this and that, and though he's not the cheapest on the block, his stock is never short of Grade-A merchandise.

Oh, and yeah, I've taken on the Vargas job … despite knowing full well I'm walking into a fucking viper's nest of trouble.

THE SILVER STEED EMPORIUM

My meeting with Zheng was as cordial as usual. I'm a fan, and I know he's cool with me too. I snagged a few upgrades for my safe zone, and a sweet sharp I can conceal real easy. My Magnum-Drive now has enough ammo for a small nation conflict and I even picked up a frequency disruptor I can deploy from the Grav. It's always a pleasure doing business with him, but now I'm en route to drop in on an old buddy from my service days. When the war was done, many of us took advantage of the cheap real estate that was up for grabs. James Templeton Danzig, or JT as we called him, did exactly that. That wily bastard built himself a sweet little empire from the ashes of old Tokyo, and now he's sitting pretty with enough time on his hands to indulge his true passion: motorcycles. He actually owns a few antique pieces of Americana which were salvaged from their respective graveyards in the old country and lovingly restored.

His club is a thing of wonder. Those antiques are dotted around the place and the style of the whole is steeped in American history. Flags of every state from the old union hang from the rafters and design references from way back in the frontier days lend that air to it. Sure, it's not that much different from many other establishments set up by us

Westerners, but there's something just right about the ambience of the spot. Of course, the fact that JT's 'motorcycle' gang operate out of the back rooms may just be another reason why I'm drawn to the outlaw feel of the Silver Steed Emporium. It's always good seeing that custom chrome cruiser he's got parked above his front door, and the sights, sounds, and smells of the place just add to the authenticity. The air's always thick with smoke and the scent of hard liquor, and I'm just right at home in the danger there.

Parked up, I drift in and get scoped by strangers and some of JT's crew who give me the nod as I take my time on the sweeping staircase which spills you into the subterranean den. I've witnessed many a bust-up here. These steps got a bloody history to them. But they've also got game, in that they've lured a ton of unsuspecting punters into parting with far too much money.

The built-in-a-cave feel gives it a killer vibe and you feel as though you're entering a forbidden hive the authorities have constantly got eyes on. And they do have eyes on it. Not bugs, cause JT sweeps this place on a regular basis. I'd bet all my stash, though, that a few of the guys giving me the eye as I make my way down are underworld spies keeping tabs on JT's business. He'll know it too and will simply play the fuckers in any number of ways.

I hear that bawdy laugh of his above the general noise and I follow it to a booth in the games room, where he's having another laser-fire tattoo branded onto his weathered hide.

He's got his back to me and the volume level on the audio system is way up, but I guess those old instincts are just hardwired. Without looking up, or missing a beat, he offers me a welcome.

"How long's it been?"

I make the sweep around to stand in front of him and I give him a 'fuck if I know' shrug. He grins through the smoke from that fat cigar he's puffing away on and the mouthful of gold teeth twinkle.

"Balaam Hendrix, you concrete motherfucker … how the hell are ya?"

The tattoo artist gives neither one of us a second and stays focused on the job.

"Oh, y'know … getting soft and all sentimental these days."

He laughs so much he starts to choke on the cigar smoke and gestures to the skin fixer it's a wrap for the day.

"Fuck … I really ought to give these up," he says, making reference to the old-style smoke.

He gets up and gives me a bear hug which threatens to cut off my circulation, then shouts over to the barman to bring the best rum in the house. I take the seat opposite as we sit and he just grins at me like I've handed him the keys to a one hundred and fifty-year-old Harley-Davidson.

"So, Peaches, you look like shit. You eating properly?"

I roll my eyes and take my hat off. "I'm eating my leafy greens, Grandma," I assure him.

He winks. "Glad to hear it."

Now that we've got the bullshit out of the way and Encino has brought us our bottle, we can get to it. JT pours the drinks and I name drop on my current job. He stops momentarily and gives me that look of his, before adding the mixer and ice.

"Sweet Jesus … you always get into bed with the dirtiest of whores. Fucking Vargas? Seriously? Oh man, you've got a fucking death wish, I swear."

We leave that all hanging there for a while until he comes around to just dealing with it. I take a slug and give him no acknowledgement.

"I'm all ears," he declares, puffing on his cigar and folding his arms.

"It's swell 'n all that you're looking out for me, Captain. I get all choked up that you care, but I can handle myself out there."

He looks at me. "Keep quipping, wise-ass."

"Look, it's a big-money arrangement and I'm not getting any younger."

"You can't spend a penny of it, if it never reaches your pocket in the first place."

I hear what he's saying.

"He'll sell you down the river, my friend. Won't even think twice about it. He'll assume his private army is enough to protect him."

Truth be told, I've already thought of all that, but the assets he's wanting back will be the ace up my sleeve.

"I'm not assigned to dust anyone. He wants his property back and the employee who took it."

He ponders that, then seems to loosen up a little. "So that's your leverage, yeah? Played in two halves I'll wager? He only gets all the goods when you get the final payday."

"Sure, and when we exchange I'll have my own private army on hand."

He frowns, takes a slug, and then the penny drops.

"That'll mark my card with him. That's a big ask, my friend."

"I know … so you can name your price."

I drain my glass and refill it and he declines my offer of a top-up.

He's chewing it over. It reminds me of our days on the front line when he had all those weighty decisions to make.

"Y'know, it occurs to me I owe you one anyways," he comes back with.

Whatever it is, it escapes me, and so he simply gets a blank look. He notes my vague expression and explains.

"It was a total clusterfuck … but then again, what wasn't in that god-awful mess? We were under almost continual bombardment and completely cut off from our supply lines. There was a fuck-almighty weather front which sat over us for three days, and not only were we cut to pieces, but we were drenched in misery too."

It's a blur, as most of what I recall seems that way. He sees I'm still not at the parade and so I get the rest of it.

"Doesn't surprise me. When they put you back together I'm sure they left out pieces of your brain. Stands to reason there's a black hole between your ears."

He gets his refill now, and when he's done, rolls up his sleeve and shows me the result of a phosphor burn from wrist to bicep. "Why do you think I've got so many tattoos? It ain't because I'm overly fond of them. I figure one burn hides another. Last I remember our position was being overrun, and I saw it all upside down before I drifted off. You carried me through a rain of hellfire and got my ass to salvation. That battleground would've been my end if it hadn't been for you. So I figure it'll make us even."

It's a fragment. Nothing more. I can't join the dots so I'll just take it as gospel.

"That was war. That's what we did. It was our code. You don't owe me a goddamn thing, JT."

"The hell I don't. I'm sitting here in my own little kingdom because of you, brother. I figure that about gives me reason enough to wear Vargas's scorn for a while."

"Besides, I wouldn't give up the opportunity of seeing that rodent nose of his all out of joint," he adds.

I grin my appreciation and we settle on our agreement with a clink of the glasses.

"So what's your next move?" he prompts.

I use the link on the armrest of the seat I'm in and access my Grid account. The holo-page springs into life between us and I punch in to bring up the mug shot and details of my mark. I flip it so JT can read it, and wait for any insight.

He runs his fingers through his shoulder-length hair to get it out of his eyes. He's greying at the temples, but he's in good shape for a man in his fifties. The Corps tattoo we both have sits across his upper right arm and the rest of the sleeves are a riot of biker graffiti. Those gold tombstones in his maw make him look like a cyborg, but one with a very human history. He rubs his goatee with a handful of scrap metal that adorns each finger and then takes another slug of liquid fire.

"This worthless piece of shit run off to a different camp?"

"He ghosted a little over three weeks ago. Vargas thinks he's still in the city, but that's about it. No idea what the fuck the weasel's doing."

He takes that in and then offers me something I'd not considered yet.

"Y'know, just about every rat in this city will know that Vargas is hunting this guy. There won't be a single soul he can count on. Rats'd give up their own mother for the reward Vargas is offering, and the guy knows it. Whatever sanctuary he's gone to, it'll be ironclad. Maybe the Soul Syndicate or one of the other crackpot cults we've got here."

He stops as he sees my slight smirk.

"What?"

"Oh, nothing."

He looks through the holo-page at me and I can see he's thinking back through what he's just said.

"Word on the street is one of those crazy bastards got himself decapitated a few days back. I suppose you've heard anyways?"

"Let's just say I had firsthand intel on that."

He gives me his best 'no fucking way' look. "You insane genius, Balaam … I can't fucking believe you did that. But then again, it's got 'you' written all over it. I'll be a son of a gun."

A golden grin splices his lips and he raises his glass in tribute.

"Ammo costs," I deliver deadpan.

He leans back in his seat and belly laughs the place down.

"Oh man, that's priceless. You're a force of nature, brother … a force of nature."

He stares at me for a second and I collapse the holopage.

"Where are you gonna start looking for this guy?"

"I don't know yet, but it'll be easier knowing you got my back."

He nods, but doesn't add anything and I get the vibe he's given me everything he has on this.

"How's the Danzig empire?" I ask, changing the subject.

"Oh, y'know … fingers in many pies as always."

He grins again and I reach across the table for a handshake. His grip is steel and I know his pledge is solid.

"Always a pleasure, JT. Be seeing ya."

He flicks a lazy salute and I'm on my way out, thinking of my next move.

***

The city is vast. On a hunt, sometimes it's hard knowing where to begin. But people make a city smaller. One guy only has so many connections. Start with those, and sooner or later, you'll get your mark. I go down my list. Friends, none. Women, no idea. Family, nada. If he has any here, he won't be in touch with them. Not that he'll much care about them. A 'ghost' like this only cares about his own hide. But he knows Vargas will be watching any family closely, and he won't take that risk, not if he has any smarts. I decide to start with his residence. In short order, I'm heading to his place, over at Harbour Heights.

A sentinel drone engages my comms as I approach that airspace and demands a stationary hold until clearance is authorised. I recite my licence number and after a few seconds it asks what business I have in the zone. It would've been nice to have that frequency disruptor I picked up from Zheng this morning already installed, but I'll have it rigged for next time. I give the sentinel a boiled down version and I'm put on hold until it makes its check with the Vargas fraternity. A few seconds more and I've got my clearance, and I look for a spot where I can set down. The secure complex is one of the most manicured I've seen and the apartment building is dotted with high-end Gravs on its numerous aero-pads. I've no idea which bay is dedicated to his accommodation, so I drop to ground level and park in a guest gravity area.

Clearly, I'm not the usual kind of visitor this place is used to, judging by the looks I'm getting, as I make my way to the lobby. It's all 'high class and laundered money' here, and I'm carrying off that 'bullets in the Bronx' look. I've got no time for these vacuous fucks and so they get my very best 'eat shit' stare. The reception hub flares into life and the in-house security turd looks me up and down. I flash my hunter shield and he unlocks the door. Inside, I give the necessary details and he tells me it's on Floor 65 as he hands me the entry bypass chip. I'll be back with questions I tell him and he doesn't seem unduly fazed by that. The elevator is the high-speed air propulsion type and it gets me to the floor before I can finish taking the safety off my Mag and readjust my hat. It's all quiet on the corridor and I drift along until I'm outside the apartment.

A thought occurs to me and I reach inside my coat for the Grid-link I always carry. I couple it up to the bypass chip and download the data on it. It's done in seconds, and so I stow the device and put the chip into the door's security interface. It runs the sequence and I'm in. Gun in hand, I make a wary entrance.

There's no evidence any of Vargas's goons were here. I can smell the odour of cleaning fluid, so the place has been mopped up. I grab my SpectraSpecs from my inside pocket, put them on, and study the room in ultraviolet. I tell the eco-system to close all the shutters, and as the light dies, I see some small spatters of blood that got missed by the cleaners. They seem to lead from the bathroom to the armchair in the day room.

Before I even set foot in the wash area it's obvious someone got roughed up in there and dragged to the chair. When I instruct the lights to come on and remove the glasses I see the slightly botched handiwork of a replacement piece of glass in the mirrored cabinet above the sink. Done in haste I'd say, as it's a poor job of disguising the damage. I'm guessing Treece got his nose introduced to it before being hauled into that chair. I put my eyewear on the resin countertop and collect the minute samples I need off the floor and unit panels.

Done in the bathroom, I pocket the evidence and eyewear and get the shutters hauled up throughout the space to let the daylight flood back in. So, whoever it was, got dragged to that armchair over there and sat down for a 'talking to.' Vargas kept real quiet about that. I wonder what else he's not telling me? My instincts tell me 'a whole truckload,' but I'll probably only ever find out half of it. Question is, was it my mark or someone else? It doesn't stack up as automatic that just because it's his apartment that he was the one who got knocked around.

The blood's a good start, but I know that if it's Treece's it won't flag up on analysis. He's a ghost—no DNA profile anywhere, so I need something else to make this sweep totally worthwhile. There's some personal effects dotted around the place. The kinda stuff you don't need when you're planning to disappear. Then there's a stack of clothes you can't take with you when you're travelling light. I diligently go through pockets and come up empty handed.

There's no framed photographs of Waylon Treece, or indeed of anyone else. I know it's old fashioned, but it's still how a lot of people personalise their space. I go through every drawer, cabinet, and walk-in closet, just as I'm sure Vargas's foot soldiers did. Nothing: nada: zip. Along the adjoining wall in the day room there's something I've not seen in a very long time. Three bookshelves populated with actual books. Shit, this stuff is rare these days, so the whole collection must be worth a song.

There's probably about five hundred titles sitting here and I've not got the time, nor the inclination, to flick through them all. I'm going to take a gamble, on a hunch, and go for some at standing height. I figure if there are any which my mark has handled lately it'll be one of those. I scan along my line of sight and come to rest on the only title which has a very small amount of a bookmark on show at its top edge.

It's a book called *The Master Key: An Electrical Fairy Tale* by L. Frank Baum, and it's a hardcover with a worn dust jacket. The bookmark's sitting at page 57 and so I take the time to read its contents, in the hopes it'll throw up something meaningful. Again, nothing. I don't get a big wet kiss to my brain and go to slam the book shut, which tips the bookmark out and it lands face down on the floor. It's a tatty old card type with what looks like actual pencil markings on the back of it. Hell, a pencil must be just about the rarest thing in the whole of NeuTokyo these days. What I can only assume is my mark's handwriting, reads: I wonder what they put in CTs? That's the kiss I was hoping for. Whatever it means, it's lost on me, but I know for sure it'll mean something to someone. I put the title back in its spot and hang on to the marker.

I've hit saturation point with this place and so I quit as I'm sure the apartment has given up its story. I hand the bypass chip to the guard when I'm back down below. Inside the Chrysler, I put in a comms call to an acquaintance and tell him to be ready when I head in with the blood sample. Provided it's not from my mark, or any other 'ghost,' he'll be able to match the DNA profile to someone I can go calling on. Inside an hour of dropping it off, my Grid account gets a notification on the information I need and I pull the Grav out of traffic to access the report. The usual fee token is attached and so I pay it straight off to dismiss it. The holo-page springs up from the Grav's console, displaying the lowdown on one Ivy Leigh Mayer. There's an uptown address and she's not flagged as deceased, so I turn my buggy around and set my sights on Chinatown.

When the empire crushed Japan's last stand, an entire district of the city was flattened to make way for the invaders to put their stamp of authority on it. But, there's also a flipside here, in that the clandestine aura of this place makes it that much harder to crack when it comes to getting information. Even my badge and licence give me no advantage, as there's no real judicial system other than a loose accord open to manipulation.

Meyer's not home when I arrive, but I catch a lucky break. As I'm about to leave, a janitor emerges from a maintenance duct. I know from personal experience that janitors are a great source of intel. A little money in his palm and I learn Meyer works at the Coiled Serpent club, taking care of high-class clients. I thank the janitor and I'm on my way.

Getting into the Coiled Serpent won't be easy. I'll have to negotiate entry, and places like that tend to protect their own. When I arrive, I step out of the Chrysler and head to the twin dragon statues flanking the door. As I approach, a hatch opens in the door and a voice speaks to me in broken English, asking me why I'm there.

"I'm here to see Ivy."

"Ivy not here. You come back tomorrow, Reverend."

"How about I stand in the lot here all day and when it begins to fill up with your wealthy clientele, I give them something to worry about?"

The hatch slides shut and it's about a minute or so before it reopens. This time it's a different voice which quizzes me.

"What do you want?" asks a female I'm assuming is her.

"We need to have a little chat about Treece."

There's a pause and the hatch closes again, only this time it's followed by the door being unlocked and swung open.

"You'd best come in, as this looks bad for the club," she points out.

She's about 5' 6" and has that feline prowl thing down to a fine art as she leads me to the back rooms where we can talk. She's not a natural blonde and I'm guessing the expensive dress and heels she's got on belong to the club. Two gorillas shadow us all the way, but I pay them no mind and they lose interest in me. They peel off as we reach the staff room and three others inside disappear as she makes it clear we need some privacy. She takes a seat and looks every bit the little girl she's trying so hard to mask in the company of grown-ups.

"So ... you and Treece?"

She finally looks me in the face and I can just make out the trauma to the bridge of her nose which hasn't finished healing yet, beneath the cover-up cosmetic she's wearing.

"Waylon was just a client. We had some good times but now that's over."

I keep my gaze neutral. Give her nothing to pick up on.

"Those good times include smashing your face into his bathroom mirror?" Her eyes look into mine and then away. "Yeah, I found your blood there. What happened?"

She shifts a little in her seat and I up the tension a gear. Leaning forward, I whisper so the room's listening devices temporarily lose my questioning.

"If you think Vargas was rough on you keep going, sister. I'll shoot the fuck out of this place and drag your ass to somewhere I can make this interrogation last a whole lot longer."

Pathetic defiance rears its head.

"You won't make it past the front door," she spits.

I lean in a little further. "There won't be a fucking front door when I'm finished, sweetheart. You'll be starting to get the idea I'm fucking serious right about now I'm guessing, so let me just point out there isn't a tombstone in NeuTokyo which reads: I got one over on The Reverend."

In a way, I admire the fact she's trying to protect Treece, but what's coming is unstoppable. She seems to look even smaller than she was when we started this, as the body language has gone all submissive.

"I was there … Waylon had set me up on the security system to have access. He told me he needed to lay low for a while. I was only there clearing out the last of my belongings when Vargas showed up with his entourage. They thought I knew where he'd gone, but I know about as much as anybody," she says through tears.

I lean back and study her. Now I'm getting the truth.

"So there's nothing you can tell me that will pinpoint his whereabouts?"

She just shakes her head and backhands the tears away.

I think for a moment before reaching inside my overcoat and take the bookmark out of the pocket. She frowns at it and it's obvious it means nothing to her.

"There's something written on this and I need you to take a look at it."

With that, I pass it across the table. Having read it, she frowns again and looks blank on handing it back.

"You've got nothing?"

She shrugs with a genuine lack of knowledge.

Fuck. I thought if anyone would know, she would. I just stare at her and say nothing for about a full minute and then get up to go.

"You're going to kill him, aren't you?"

"Treece? No, my job is to bring him in alive so Vargas can mete out punishment."

She momentarily looks at the floor and seems to relax a little in the revelation.

"I've given it some thought … and I think I know what the question means," she adds.

I put my hands on the table and lean across. "Go on."

I think it's dawned on her he's somewhere I can't get to him and so she's happy to have me waste my time on the trail.

"I think he was wondering what they put in Chromium Teardrops."

Virtually Non-existent

Y'know it's funny, I've never once paid any attention to those annoying ads that appear all over the city. Morning, noon, and night, one-thousand-foot photo-neon billboards run the same thing over and over again. Some digging on the Spectre Grid reveals the company I've got my sights on has been running for eight years now. It's strange, but it feels like forever and a day that I've seen their kooky promotions and wondered what the fuck that crap was all about. The company in question is V-Trance Industries, or VTI as their logo depicts. It's a French entity masterminded by Jean-François Baptiste. I recall some early-day horror stories of the odd customer having their mind fried for the privilege, but since then, there's been nothing. SIN: THETICA they call it.

I'd wrongly assumed it was some pharmaceutical brand in the first few months of seeing the ads, as I'd paid very little attention to it. There's a million and one stories kicking around telling of some rather seedy experiences being had in their trance factory. I guess it's like anything of that nature. You put a twisted individual in there and they're gonna live out their sordid little fantasies. I'm sure that isn't true for most who go in there, and it seems my man Treece has done exactly that.

It makes perfect sense, and JT's words rattle around in my head as if to hammer home the obvious. It's the only sanctuary he'd have been able to find in this hateful city. I've been at this straight since early morning and so I've stopped off at my safe zone to eat something and do some research on Baptiste's baby before I head on over there. It's nice to enjoy a cigar and it somehow seems a sweet little reward for the plays I've made so far.

The Grid data maps out something along the lines of an alternative reality being peddled by VTI, but it's not very specific. I know from snippets I've picked up here and there that the CTs are somehow linked to the process, but exactly how I'm not sure. I collapse the holo-page I'm looking at and get some food onboard. This is a bit chewy whatever it is. It's supposed to be duck but I'm betting it's rat. These food companies are a bunch of fucking liars who just buy their way out of trouble. It's been a productive half day, but I have to figure a way around VTI's confidentiality clause to get a solid answer on Treece's movements. I might just have to roll the dice and put my gun in someone's mush to get a result.

It's raining again as I set off for an uninvited drop-in on the trance factory. It's the rainy season and it's going to do this almost constantly for months. It makes me think briefly about global history. We'd rotted away the Earth's atmospheric skin and the brainiacs eventually came up with a solution after the sun's rays had caused scars for decades. They say we turned things around, but I'm not so sure about that, as I can't recall a time when things weren't fucked up. The French Quarter looms now and I've always found its atmosphere a strange one. Every time I've set foot there I've met with a more stubborn resistance to my trade than anywhere else. Maybe they hate the weight of my profession, or maybe it's just me and my methods.

Whatever the case, it's fine by me, as I fucking hate them too.

VTI HQ has an almost fortress-like facade, and instead of the automated sentinels most companies adopt for security, Baptiste has opted for a human force fully kitted out with the very latest in tech. I guide the Grav to the bay on the entry tower and the armoured grunt behind the view port gives me a visual instruction to land. The comms flare to life and they want to know what business I have here.

"Do you have an appointment?"

"No."

"The company doesn't accept unscheduled visits, you'll have to leave."

"I need to see Baptiste. Now. It can't wait."

"And you are?"

A swipe of the comms sends my licence data through and I wait. I can see him exchange a look with grunt number two who walks into view, and then I'm put on hold. The company's gigantic logo atop the central building spins in slow rotation, filling my windshield with a skewed version of its neon output, which shrinks to nothing in a conical collapse as it momentarily turns out of view. In seconds it's back again, as if to remind the viewer of its ever-present dominance of this district's skyline.

"Monsieur Baptiste is a very busy man, you'll have to make an appointment through the accepted channels."

The fuck I will.

"Give Baptiste this name: Vargas."

The two hired hands exchange another look and I'm put on hold again. I take a look through the quarter light over my shoulder and see inside the complex. It's a limited view, but I glimpse row upon row of privately owned transport docked in individual bays. The heavy downpour makes it hard to see specifics, but it's obvious the 'money people' are its primary source of revenue. The Gravs are all pretty much top of the line and I can see the odd glow here and there from the automated valets which are cleaning the interiors of a handful in the lot. I'm guessing that's ahead of some scheduled departures.

"You've got clearance. Follow the docking lights to Bay 7 in Sector C. Someone from Monsieur Baptiste's personal entourage will meet you there and talk you through procedures. Be prepared to surrender your weapons, bounty hunter."

Yeah. Fuck you.

I give him zero acknowledgement, and put the Grav into gear, nearly hitting the barrier he has to raise at speed to avoid a collision. The tower hails me as I pass through, undoubtedly to reprimand me, but I ignore the fuckers by switching my comms off. Rattling into the docking bay I see a woman standing beyond the coupling plates who looks like she just stepped in shit in her shiny new shoes. Yeah, I get that look a lot, but they always get that attitude back tenfold, so who's going to win that pithy little contest? She's all 'power suit and powder' and I just want to throw up. This should be interesting. Out of the vehicle, she waits until I've cleared the distance on the gantry before offering a faux friendly greeting.

"Mr. Hendrix. What an unexpected pleasure."

"Yeah, I bet first thing this morning the very thought going through your head was 'gee, wouldn't it be swell to have afternoon tea with a cold-hearted killer today'."

The change in body language says it all, and resisting the urge to return my vitriol with equal zeal, she gets down to business.

"Follow me. Don't deviate from the path. When we reach the checkpoint, hand your weapon to the guard. Don't try to conceal anything when you go through the scanner. Do not attempt to record audio or video while here. Any breach of security will be dealt with. With prejudice. Let's go."

With that, she flashes me an icy look, turns on her heels, and we head off.

At the checkpoint, she turns her back to me and types something into the holo-page from her hyper-link bracelet, whilst waiting for me to disarm and pass my inventory to the sentry. When done, we carry on down a long corridor. She's mid-twenties, and given the accent, English. I'm guessing she's Baptiste's personal assistant.

"And the nature of that report you just made to Baptiste was what exactly?"

Again, the icy look, but no explanation.

The space is all black marble and diffused lighting and reminds me of long walks through military facilities. Business and the Corps are similar anyways, so I guess it's not that much of a stretch. The corridor's got a 'tech room' temperature and I'm thinking the rest of the place will be exactly the same. We pass what appear to be booths of some description but I can't tell whether they're occupied or not. After a couple of turns we take the elevator three levels down and exit into a sprawling reception that's all smoked glass, chromium, and vibrant green plant life. There's an aroma here too that I can't pinpoint. Whatever it is irritates my throat a tad.

A receptionist sits flanked by security personnel and all three eye me with disdain as I approach the desk. I know ahead of meeting Baptiste he'll not act the same way, as he'll be all fake smiles and vacuous hospitality, just like his assistant here. We go through the routine and this is where 'Miss English' disappears and I'm escorted by the two stiffs to Baptiste's empty office. The pair take up positions either side of the door and I'm left to take a seat and wonder just when exactly their head honcho is going to make an appearance. His office is more like a palatial pad than a working environment. Everything's tech and opulence, giving me a sense of the man before I even meet him.

Sure enough, when he eventually shows his face, he's everything I'd pictured he'd be. Calculated charm. Effete manner. The air of a man whose work is so important you'd think he was busy building the next fucking Roman Empire. He merely nods in my direction on entering, instructing the guards to leave. He's cocksure he won't need them. Just another thing I hate about him already. Tall, well-built, and I'd say … mid-thirties, the kind of handsome successful bastard you'd just simply want to punch out of sheer jealousy if you're someone who's bothered by all that. Me? I'm not, as I've got everything I want in this fucked up world … save wife and child.

"Mr. Hendrix. What can we do for Mr. Vargas?"

He asks this as he takes a seat beyond the low glass table between us and gestures to the refreshments on it. I pass and put my hat on my lap, and get straight to it because I don't want to spend any more time in his presence than is necessary.

"All my intel says a Vargas employee is currently in suspension here. And, given said asshole stole something from my current employer, I need to bring him out."

"Ah, I see. That does pose a problem, Mr. Hendrix."

He leans back in his chair and gathers his thoughts.

"Here at VTI, client confidentiality is the backbone of our code and while I'm sympathetic to Mr. Vargas's plight I'm afraid we cannot breach our protocol under any circumstances. It's a legal obligation. Mr. Vargas will just have to understand."

He says it in a way which brings to mind how an adult speaks to a child when telling them why they can't have what they want. And then there's the other aspect of this too, the whole legal jargon line, which is plain rich in light of the fact NeuTokyo is the most lawless place in the Asia-Pacific.

"What judicial system are we talking about exactly? Would that be the one where anyone with enough wealth can buy whatever outcome they want? You're looking at the hand of the law, Baptiste, and it really doesn't get any more complex than that."

He looks at the floor briefly before answering. "In the corporate world things aren't really so simplistic, Mr. Hendrix. Granted, NeuTokyo is, as you say, governed in a very questionable way and so as such is open to much manipulation."

"So VTI's pockets are the real issue, yes?"

He smiles a little.

"SIN:THETICA is profit, Mr. Hendrix. We have investors to consider and believe me they are far more powerful and connected than your Mr. Vargas. No offence intended."

He says that like I give a fuck about what Vargas might think.

"So your trance factory harbours criminals and you operate with impunity. That's the real world behind the fake one you offer."

"You're breaking my heart, Mr. Hendrix. A man of your profession is surely used to life's harsh realities, no?"

You have no idea, you fucking weed.

It's my turn to smile a little.

"I don't give a fuck about your profits or your investors."

His demeanour changes a little. "You're sounding a little threatening, Mr. Hendrix. If I were you, I'd tread very carefully."

I simply raise an eyebrow.

"I can have security here in a matter of seconds. Any heavy-handedness on your part won't turn out to be profitable for either yourself or your Mr. Vargas."

I grin. It tells him on any given day I'm just crazy enough to test that theory. It seems to make an impression.

He uses the silence between us to re-evaluate the situation.

"It would seem we've gotten off on the wrong foot, Mr. Hendrix. Let's see if there's a middle ground we can reach."

I nod, then get to it.

"My mark is one Waylon Treece. He crossed Vargas and so his former boss wants retribution. He simply has to be brought in."

Baptiste frowns a little.

"If you want to take your man in alive you simply can't remove him from stasis. You see, when a subject is immersed in SIN:THETICA their bodies are in limbo in order to preserve bio-functions. It takes time to bring subjects out of that. Taking your man, if indeed he's here, out of immersion without the proper extraction methods will leave him in a coma, and I'm sure your Mr. Vargas will be most unimpressed by that."

He seems to relish this little nugget of knowledge.

"How long?"

"Typically a subject takes a week to recover. However, there are no hard and fast rules when it comes to withdrawal. We see subjects who recover sooner and others who take twice as long. It really depends on the individual and their ability to readjust."

He knows I don't have that amount of time and I bet he's thinking 'fuck you, Hendrix.' This is a truckload of ball ache and walking away from the whole deal is suddenly looking real attractive right now. I've given a day of my time to this so far, so if I cut my losses and tell Vargas I've drawn a blank, I can pick up something else within days and keep the money rolling in. I'll make an enemy of Vargas though, and that might prove a bad move in the long run. In the few seconds it's taken me to ponder this, I know Baptiste is reading the situation. He'll realise it puts me in a shitty position and no doubt he'll be gloating inside.

"Let me suggest something, Mr. Hendrix. But first we must determine whether or not your man is indeed immersed in our programme."

He brings up a holo-screen, runs a search, and it brings up Treece's profile.

"It seems your detective work is flawless. We do indeed have Mr. Treece housed in Suite Five."

Collapsing the page, he takes a moment to consider VTI's position no doubt. "This might seem like a radical proposal but please hear me out, Mr. Hendrix. As explained, extraction is not a simple process and therefore it might be better to consider a second immersion in this case."

"A second what?"

"Immersion. Rather than Mr. Treece come out, you go in."

What ... the ... fuck?

"No fucking way you're plugging me into your head grinder. I'm here to take a man out, not put myself into some fucked-up cerebral circus."

He flat out laughs and it stops me in my tracks.

"Why, Mr. Hendrix, I do believe we've discovered your Achilles heel. It's quite endearing that a man of your background should be scared of such a small process like SIN:THETICA. Don't worry, I won't tell a soul."

Normally, I'd have slammed this motherfucker before he'd finished that comment, but I'm kind of hanging by my balls right now. He's not wrong. The idea of going under just screams vulnerability at me and I just can't put myself in a position like that. Besides, what's the point? I can't get into Treece's private party, so it's not as if it's worth a shot anyway.

"I'm not scared of your big neon nightmare, Baptiste. Even if I agree to this I've got no way of getting inside Treece's own little world. From what I imagine, everyone has their own personal trip. I'd be just as far away from him in there as I am out here."

He grins a little and slowly wags a finger.

"Ah, but that is where you're wrong, Mr. Hendrix. SIN: THETICA isn't some fantasy playground in which an individual's psyche is free to create whatever elaborate construct they wish. There are rules and fundamental boundaries which govern the alternate reality. The NeuTokyo we see all around us is the same NeuTokyo beyond the wall of consciousness. The process builds what is perceived from daily experiences acquired over the lifetime of the subject. A learning matrix reads their subconscious and replicates that architecture. Just think, Mr. Hendrix. Many thousands of the city's inhabitants have immersed themselves in the programme since inception. Each brain is a memory bank which uploads its data to the replication pool."

Pausing, he takes a sip of water.

"When first realised, and brought online, the engine at the heart of the system was fed a steady stream of data corresponding to every conceivable piece of information about the city. Infrastructure, culture, history, districts, businesses, domiciles, trends, and lifestyles. You name it—the list is endless. And all of it, every single piece that can be thought of, is constantly updated by the data feeds that run night and day, and all of it augmented by the next individual to be plugged in."

"What you have is a reality as real as any you've experienced, in a world of familiarity. The only thing that's different is the path you take through the maze, so to speak. Meaning, you can't alter your perception of the world around you but you can make different choices, and therefore experience an alternate life to the one you live right now."

I'm trying to process all that but some of it's a bit slippery. A cigar will help, so I reach inside my coat, snag one, and move to light it up.

"I'm afraid you can't smoke that here, Mr. Hendrix. There are strict safety measures applied to VTI's working environment."

I light it anyway.

"Then let's just say I'm altering my perception of the world around me, Baptiste."

Mere seconds later, my cigar is disintegrated by a laser which springs out of nowhere and I'm left with ash all over my crotch.

"By all means light another, Mr. Hendrix. And another after that if you wish. Our systems will keep you on the right side of healthy all day long. I did warn you."

He's amused at my stunned expression.

I dust the ash off and continue the conversation.

"I still don't see the point of going in. I need to take Treece to Vargas, so what exactly will going in achieve?"

"I'm glad you ask. Sure, you'll not be able to extract your man, but you will be able to question him. The answers you'd get would be as real as any you'd get on the outside, as you'd be dealing with Treece's mind either way."

"I've already tracked him down once. I assume I'd have to do it again?"

"Undoubtedly."

He takes another sip of water.

"How long have you been looking for him?"

"It took me half a day to track him here."

"Then there's no real need to put you under for very long, Mr. Hendrix. If you were in say … forty-eight hours, it'd take about four hours to recover. A short stasis wouldn't require anything other than to keep your body hydrated for the duration. Of course, you'd be quite hungry on waking, but nothing a square meal wouldn't fix. You'd be in and out in two and a half days, and you'd have some answers for your Mr. Vargas."

When I woke this morning none of this crazy rat shit was on my agenda, so it's fucking with my head right now. He gets up, walks to a door at the far side and slides it open to bring in some air from the open balcony beyond. Standing in the doorway, he continues his pitch.

"This is the only thing I can offer you. You see, everything is logged here, and any deviation from protocol would result in an investigation. The footage we have of you in your time here, and the audio too like this conversation, would be analysed and used in the company's case against you. You said it yourself, Mr. Hendrix. Those with enough money buy the outcomes they require, so I'll remind you that our backers are more wealthy and influential than your current employer."

He's right, but all this doesn't add up to shit if I simply back off and drop the job into a thousand-foot hole in the ground.

"There's something I don't understand, Baptiste. Treece had written something which led me here in the first place … something about Chromium Teardrops."

He turns and looks out across the district.

"They're a physical connector to SIN:THETICA. They have the look of mercury. We place a drop in each eye before immersion and their make-up acts as a neural magnet which anchors the subject's mind to the software."

He turns back to me.

"Think of them as harmless eye drops. Nothing to be concerned about, I assure you."

This is all sounding like a screwed-up eighth grade science project. Why didn't I just stick to jobs that only require me to put a hole where someone's head used to be? So far, no one knows I'm here and Vargas won't be expecting any report from me for at least a few days. I need time to think. Right now, it's just too much to take in, and the idea of being in the hands of Baptiste's pseudo-scientists is about as appealing as a one-night stand with a leper.

I put my hat back on and get up. He doesn't move from the doorway and simply watches me head for the exit.

"I take it we're done, Mr. Hendrix?"

"Maybe."

I stop and look over my shoulder.

"I gotta go think this one through, and I think best with rum in my veins. I'll let you know, Baptiste."

***

Back at the Grav I can't help wondering how much I've been lied to. There's a feeling I can't shake and I always trust that feeling. Would I tell me everything if I was in his shoes? Probably not, so as long as I know that going into this then I can handle the fallout. With VTI in the rear view I head for my safe zone and pick up supplies on the way. I suddenly remember the copy of the security log I made at Treece's apartment and make a mental note to go through the data when I get back. After foodstuffs, last on my list are more cigars and rum, and so I land the Grav outside Ma Tsingtao's place and head on in. The wave of exotic aromas hits straight away and her Macaw, Cyrus, lets her know I've arrived.

"Here's Hendrix. Watch your back, Ma. Watch your back."

"Funny bastard … you should have your own show."

I give him a monkey nut from the stash Ma keeps under the counter and tell him to choke on it. She's out back, and the sounds of her clattering around spill through into the storefront. It's empty, save me and 'numb nuts' here, so I take a minute to cast an eye around before she emerges.

Ma's one of those old girls who's seen just about everything come and go in NeuTokyo over the years. I've got a soft spot for her as she's kinda like the grandma I never knew. Saying that, she's a tough old bird to boot and keeps the under counter stocked with enough stopping power to drop a small army.

I guess I like that sweet and sour flavour to her character, and you've just gotta respect an ageing dame who keeps an old school Remington pump action to hand. She calls it her TAC—a reference to the models back in the day.

"That you, Reverend?"

She's putting her glasses on as she appears through the hanging beads that cover the back room entrance. Those things are as old as she is, so I doubt they even have me in focus.

"Hey Ma, how've you been? I ain't seen you in a while."

She smiles warmly, and comes to give me a big hug.

"Oh, you know, still breathing."

I'm being hugged a little too enthusiastically here.

"If I was thirty years younger," she whispers.

Reaching down, she pinches my ass before breaking off, and I'm not really sure how I feel about that. It's been a long day and I think I need a drink right now. Chuckling to herself as she moves behind the counter, she parks her butt on the rickety old stool there and beams at me.

"I need leaf and molasses, Ma, and I need a port order of both."

"Bad day?"

"Nah, just kinda complicated."

A box is procured from under the counter—no doubt my smokes.

"Get crate out back. I no lift," she says, gesturing.

"You got Pacific Port back there?"

"Two stacks."

I wander through into what looks like a smuggler's paradise. It never fails to impress me. From what I know, her dead husband was a man who could get you anything if the price was right. When he bought the farm, she carried on the fine tradition, and thank God she did. It's my vices that keep my head above water in this soulless place, and I'd be sunk if it wasn't for runners like Ma. A crate carries twelve bottles, and I guess that'll keep me stocked for a while. I hoist one onto my shoulder and swear I hear a slight scuffle come from the front end. She hasn't just dropped dead on me out there, has she?

"Ma, you still with me?"

No answer, and I'm about half a step from the bead curtain. Now parting it, there's two deadbeats waving hand cannons around—one aimed at her, and now the other at me.

"Wrong day to go shopping, asshole. Now slowly put that crate on the counter and keep your hands where I can see them."

Creep number one seems to think he's in charge so I ignore him and ask Ma how she's doing.

"Hey, 'Cool Fuck,' look at me. You've got about three seconds before I ..."

The front of the counter shatters as Ma discharges the Remington and he's thrown a good five feet into the aisle shelving behind. Merchandise is sent tumbling, and creep number two has about two seconds of life left before Ma brings the shotgun up from underneath.

They're now pointing their guns at each other. Both go off at the same time, but he's stumbling backwards as he fires and Ma's got the scattergun's dispersal in her favour. Turns out neither one of them can aim very well, but today lady luck is smiling on an old Chinese woman who's meaner than a Japanese fighting dog.

His round puts a hole in the wall above her left shoulder, and hers puts one in his hidden body armour. And though saved by Kevlar, his head hits the corner edging of the display unit behind him, and it's 'lights out muchacho.' A stillness follows, before she spits on the floor and slams the TAC onto the countertop.

"Motherfuckers. Look what they've done."

The place is trashed for sure, so I put the crate down and offer to tidy up.

"Not store," she screams.

I half turn and get a better look at her. Her glasses are sitting crooked on her face and the right lens has seen better days.

"My fucking glasses. Forty years I have these and now they busted long time. Fucking … cock suck … motherfuckers. I cut their balls off and have new earrings."

It's been an 'interesting' day in many ways, but I'm beyond fried right now. It's almost like I never left VTI and this whole sketch is just Baptiste and his cronies having a good laugh at the programme they've dropped me into. I ponder that for a second, and … *nah, don't even go there, Hendrix*. A quick shake of the head and I start the mop-up operation.

Ma's still muttering away as I close the front door and drag creeps one and two into the back room. She tells me to just leave the scattered stock out front as she kneels down and performs a well-rehearsed search of the pair. I'm guessing they've been busy rolling a few spots in the district, as their pockets are fairly well stacked. She's happier now as she beams at the money, and I give her a wink as I head past to pick up my goods and go.

"You no pay, lover boy. Motherfucks already paid for you," she says, waving their wads of Shanghai Dollars with glee.

She gets a nod and a grin, and I save my last word on the affair for Cyrus as I walk out the door.

"Some fucking security guard you are, 'Never Saw Macaw'."

Upon Reflection

I had every intention of checking that security log data last night, but the rum had other ideas. I'm not sure when it was that I slipped into sleep. It's after nine, and I'm starting to surface through a heady haze of Narcoplex, nicotine, and booze. A lot of thought went into the VTI quandary before I hit the sack, and so my head hurts. That's what I'm blaming it on, anyways. I need a lengthy piss, a caffeine kickstarter and a smoke to go with it.

My shoulder is aching which tells me I was lying oddly and that the effects of the Narcoplex have worn off. Post flush, I'm looking at Frankenstein's monster staring back at me from the mirror on the bathroom cabinet. I make it my morning ritual to take a good look at the wreck that is Balaam Hendrix. It keeps me grounded. It's a visual reminder that no matter how broken something is, it can always be put back together.

That's what I did after they took my girls away. It took an eternity but I got there. That doesn't mean the pain isn't still with me, it's just that it's different … less raw, but always in my shadow.

There's not a day goes by where I don't think of them. It keeps the Magnum muzzle out of my mouth—the thought that I'll get my revenge one day for what was taken from me. The architect of that misery is currently doing time in Beijing's maximum security penitentiary, so I knock each square off the calendar in a countdown towards judgement day.

I look at the surgeon's handiwork and trace the map of scars down my left side. It all starts at my ankle bone, and ends with a final splice through my eyebrow. I didn't lose the eye because of how I was thrown from the carrier. They told me it must have been a matter of mere millimetres in the shrapnel's trajectory.

The bullet wounds were an added 'fuck you,' kinda like the icing on the cake. I'm not going to win any beauty contests anytime soon but I'm fine with that. What matters is I work. I still function as a specimen, albeit with a few ailments which I know will get worse in the long run. For now, Hendrix is operational, and I just have to make the most of that. My finger goes to a few of the scars and I remember how she'd kiss them to show me they didn't matter one bit to her. I get lost in the memory of her and pull out of it by splashing my face. A lone tear is part of the water now swirling down the plughole and I've had my 'moment' for the day. Drying, I drop the towel in the laundry and grab a shirt on the way to the kitchen. With coffee in hand, and the first smoke of the day in the other, I head out onto the aero-pad and watch the urban sprawl get dizzy.

Weather permitting, I try to do this every morning. It blows the cobwebs out and helps me focus on what's in front of me. I've had a few Zen moments out here in my time. So do I chase after Treece in Baptiste's cyber-works, or do I tell Vargas to go hang? I wrestled with this all last night and a big part of it is me never ditching a job once I've agreed to it.

However, I only ever waste people and never have to bring them in, so it's not like I stuck to my code in the first place. Truth is, having Vargas as an enemy for the rest of my days is a dumb play, and that's the real problem here. At this point, I'm equal parts intrigued and traumatised by SIN:THETICA. My initial reaction was 'run a mile,' but now I've had time to process what Baptiste told me, I'm no longer dead set against it.

That in itself is probably the breakthrough moment I'm looking for and it's coming as a slow realisation. I'm still concerned about what he didn't tell me, because there'll undoubtedly be detail missing from his forced invitation. I don't like the fact he knows a shit-ton more than me about the process. That kind of advantage is how you end up screwed. And … wait a minute. Yeah, that's my Zen epiphany right there.

It's obvious now, but I guess it takes for the tornado in your skull to come full circle before you see what it's dislodged. All I have to do, between now and going in, is plug the gaps in my knowledge. There's bound to be someone, somewhere, who will know someone who's dipped their head in the replication pool. I can spend part of today talking to them and getting wise to it, and then take the plunge tonight if I'm better armed with the dirt on immersion.

Where do I start? Who's on my contacts list who might know a VTI client? Gulls are wheeling overhead and I'm wary that I'll get shit on at any moment. Now that I have a way forward to ponder, I'm going to get that data log out of the way first. Back inside, the mug gets a refill and I get to it. There's a whole month of entry and exit data on Treece's apartment log and that's going to be a bind if I have to trawl through every single movement. I see a few names come up time and again, and by their system flags they're obviously cleaning staff. Running a sweep, I eliminate them from the long list and it drops the number down to fifty-seven visitors. Hell, I don't even get that many in a year, never mind a month, but then again I'm not one of Vargas's ghosts. Why is that number screaming at me? Where have I seen it before in this whole deal?

One thing's for sure, any of the goons in Vargas's organisation won't show up on this log, as they're untraceable. Ivy Leigh Mayer's on there about the number of times that corroborates her story, but there's a whole truckload of others who are unknowns at this time. There's no pattern I can ascertain, as the days and times seem random. One thing to note is that there's comings and goings at all hours of the day, which makes me wonder when Treece actually got any sleep.

Here's where lateral thinking comes into play. I cross-correlate the times when my mark was logged as being present at the apartment with when visits took place. It rules out all but two where he wasn't. Aside from when Mayer was clearing out her belongings, and Vargas's goons showed up, it turns out the only other time is when a certain Tamsin Argyle showed up. There's roughly a six-minute time frame between her arrival and departure.

I put in a comms call to the building's security and speak to whichever stiff is on duty. On hearing my name, he recalls I quizzed him yesterday. It makes it easier to be dealing with the same face. I rattle off the date and time of Argyle's visit, and ask if there'll be footage of it. Turns out that's an easy ask, and if I give him about an hour, he'll isolate what I need and send it over. I suppose I better eat something, so having made some headway, I'll take time out and wait for the information to land.

It's probably a hangover from my Corps days, but I don't eat much first thing. I know it's bad for me, but when was the last time I did anything good? Scrambled eggs, more coffee, and another cigar, and I'm starting to feel in better shape. My man over at 'Treece Tower' is early with his reply, but that's sweet. I credit his account with a tip and he's all smiles before I break off the connection. All told, there's about one minute and seven seconds of footage, which is from the reception, an elevator, and the corridor outside the apartment door.

I pause it about three seconds into her elevator ride, as she looks up idly at the overhead camera. She's wearing shades, but I know that face. It's a small world little 'Miss English,' and it just keeps getting smaller. Baptiste's personal assistant paying Treece's apartment a visit when he ain't home—what the fuck is that all about? More to the point, the VTI guru didn't bat an eyelid when I mentioned my mark's name, yet he clearly knew of him before I showed up. That feeling I had when I left his office yesterday is barking at me now. And there's another thing—if I made a copy of the entry log then surely Vargas ordered the same. If he hasn't seen the footage I've just watched, then pigs might fly. This is starting to stink already, and I'm only a day and a half into it.

I ponder it all and decide to put in a call to Baptiste. Making contact with VTI, I'm guessing I'm through to the sour-faced receptionist I saw outside of his office.

"VTI, how may I help you?"

"Baptiste ... where is he?"

"I'm sorry, what business do you have with Monsieur Baptiste?"

"Put me on hold, and tell him The Reverend wants to speak to him in the confessional box."

She does as instructed and minutes go by.

"I'm transferring your call now, one moment please."

I've not given a second's thought to what I'm actually going to say to him. I guess I'll wait to see how he squirms.

"Ah, Mr. Hendrix, I'd not expected to hear from you so soon, given your reluctance to take up my offer yesterday."

"I love how you feign surprise when really you expected me to go away and connect the dots. When exactly were you going to drop the pretence and level with me?"

There's a pause.

"Mr. Hendrix, you have me at a loss. What exactly are you talking about?"

"How you knew about Treece before I set foot in your office."

There's another pause.

"I can assure you I did not."

"Then how come Treece's security log has your 'Miss English' at his apartment prior to him slipping into your programme?"

"I assume you're referring to Tamsin, whom you met briefly yesterday?"

"Fucking straight."

"Mr. Hendrix, Tamsin is the company's liaison and is responsible for all face-to-face contact with clients. I, on the other hand, am not the company's meet and greet service. VTI has many clients, Mr. Hendrix, with literally thousands passing through our doors in any given month. I neither have the time, nor the inclination, to cast my eye over the details of every single one who passes through our hands. SIN:THETICA's ongoing development is my key responsibility, and I'm afraid that takes up most of my time on any given day."

Slippery bastard.

"And you never heard from Vargas before I showed up?"

Yet another pause.

"No … I did not."

"Treece is one of Vargas's ghosts. There's no background to speak of. Surely that would've been flagged and brought to your attention by your very diligent Miss Argyle?"

He laughs a little, and I want to reach through the holo-page and get a chokehold on the fucker.

"We only log the information supplied to us, Mr. Hendrix. As a company, we learnt long ago not to ask too many questions. If you decide to take me up on my offer, you can call yourself Madame Knicker Elastic for all I care. In a world full of charlatans and liars it's a pointless endeavour wasting time trying to verify profiles which can easily be faked by any back-alley forger."

That makes sense. Kinda.

"So if you didn't hear from Vargas, did Miss Argyle?"

"You'll have to talk to her about that, but I'm afraid that's something which will have to wait. You see, Tamsin is unavailable at this time, as she's on annual leave right now."

That's convenient.

"And what do you know ... right after my visit yesterday."

There's that pause again.

"Mr. Hendrix, I can assure you nothing untoward has taken place. As for Miss Argyle's vacation, her request was logged some time ago and will be sitting in our company records."

I can't resist the comeback.

"Yeah, I bet. Something which can easily be faked by any back-alley forger ... or by someone with the know-how to code a very complex beast like SIN:THETICA."

There's unrestrained laughter now.

"Oh, Mr. Hendrix, I do like you. If nothing else, you're a true entertainer. I'm very much ..."

I swipe the comms and collapse the connection.

"French peacock."

If that bastard didn't know of Treece's immersion, and Vargas too, I'm a pink kangaroo.

Yeah, I said it. The reference I made to getting into a nest of vipers when I took the job. This whole thing is covered in shit, and I'm starting to reek of it too. Where was my head at when I agreed to this? I'm staring at something here but I'm just not seeing it. Time to put some pressure on Vargas.

I put in a call to that rat-faced fuck but I'm sure Baptiste will have beaten me to it, if my hunch is correct.

"Ah, Reverend, I trust you're finding all the answers in your hunt for our Mr. Treece."

"You knew about VTI but said nothing."

Vargas nods slightly, and grins like a gator. "Of course I did. Checking the security log was an obvious starting point. Let's just say I was interested in seeing how my dollars were being spent by hiring you, and I'm glad to see I've made a solid investment. A little over a day is impressive detective work, Mr. Hendrix. You are indeed living up to your reputation."

Pray I don't live up to it all the way.

"If you knew, then why not send in any of your other ghosts to flush him out? Or better still, pay Baptiste the money you're paying me to just simply give him up."

"Because it's not that simple. Baptiste may be the brains behind SIN:THETICA, but he doesn't hold the reins at VTI. He has superiors to answer to, and besides, what he earns puts him way beyond any bribe I can offer. So you see, Mr. Hendrix, the situation is complex, and if I send in any of my men I run the chance of Treece making any one of them, and going deeper into the construct to evade me."

"Why not tell me all this upfront? Why the elaborate bullshit of 'he's not left the city, blah, blah'?"

"The answer to that 'is' simple. You said it yourself. This isn't the kind of job you normally undertake. Had I talked immersion, VTI, and all that corporate bullshit, would you have been eager to come on board? No, I think not. You'll remember I asked that you indulge me a moment, so that I could take a second look at your illustrious past. Having been a soldier, you'll know it's essential to outflank your target if you're to gain the advantage. And now, having accepted my offer, you'd be unwise to renege on your contract with me."

Before he finishes what he's saying, a light has just come on in my head. His revelation is a prompt, and I now recall where I've come across the number 57 before. The bookmark was sitting at that page in the book in Treece's apartment. No doubt it was put there by Vargas to test my chops, given that it corresponds to the number of visitors through Treece's door. I'd wrongly assumed my mark had put it there, and got completely sucked in by that.

Mother … fucker. He has me by the balls.

I've always known his reputation and I shouldn't have underestimated the lengths this vampire will go to, to get what he wants.

"You put the bookmark there, right?"

"Yes, but not personally. I don't sully my hands with the particulars."

"You expect me to go in don't you."

He smirks.

"You're getting paid, Reverend. Everyone who takes my money, takes my instructions. Unless of course you intend to rip up our verbal contract?"

I hate this with every bone in my body, but I have to make it look like I'm not backed into a corner.

"I've never quit a job. You won't be granted that world first."

He grins, and I want to bust his jaw.

"Of course, you've worked out you can't extract your man from the construct?"

"Yeah, I've had that conversation. So what do you want from Treece when I find him?"

"I want the information he has and then I want you to do what you do best. Kill him inside the construct, Hendrix. He'll then be comatose inside his VTI booth, and I'll have my people take care of the clean-up operation."

What?

"So you can be ended inside SIN:THETICA?"

He looks at me like I should know that.

"So Baptiste never told you that fact … interesting. Apparently, a death within immersion is too much trauma for the subject."

"VTI will know what I've done inside their dream arena when the lights go out on Treece's monitor. I'd be wasting a man in their care, and not just on the streets. It'd be like they sanctioned it, so there's no way I can see them allowing that to happen."

"They can't stop a bounty hunter pursuing a logged assignment, and besides, I have someone on the VTI payroll in my pocket."

That light goes on in my head again.

"Let me guess. Little Miss English?"

"Oh good, Mr. Hendrix … you really are joining the dots."

"And sure as shit Baptiste doesn't know about your little arrangement."

"Absolutely, and it's within both our interests he never comes to know either. Miss Argyle will get you out when your time has expired. It's all arranged."

I still want to talk to someone who's been immersed, but I'll be damned if I'm arranging that through Vargas.

"I've got loose ends to tie up after we're done talking, but I'll be good to go this evening. I'll be wasting your ghost soon enough, Vargas."

He just smiles thinly, and I collapse the link.

***

I doubt JT will know anyone who's experienced SIN: THETICA, as he and his crew tend to keep things real. I need an option fast but my contacts list is a very specialised animal. The only one which presents a possibility is Jacks, my lab guy, and so I hail him on the Spectre Grid and wait for a reply. Back out on the aero-pad, I scatter the gulls that have gathered, light a No-Glo, and sip another refill.

I guess it was only a matter of time before I ended up being outflanked by a roach like Vargas. It's hard to see all the angles as a loner, and when you're simply trying to keep a firm footing on the shit pile, sometimes the money is all you can see. I know it blindsided me in this case, and if I come out of it in one piece, I won't be letting the dollar derail my judgement again.

My link bracelet flares and it's Jacks returning my enquiry. I drop my cigar stub on the aero-pad decking and a lone gull on my neighbour's parking space seems to think it's edible, and comes to investigate ... they really will eat anything. Back inside, I set the mug down and activate the holo-page. My lab guy is one of those typical tech types—everything behind him looks like a disorganised mess, but I bet he knows where literally everything is. Sure as hell he doesn't get out much, and as for a love life, forget it. As the page unfolds into a viewable structure, he's fiddling with something off screen, just to compound the idea his mind flips from one thing to the next like an analytical machine.

"Jacks, you got anything for me?"

"Hey Reverend ... erm, yeah, I do."

The knowledge seems to have departed and he's looking blank for a second.

"What was the question again?"

Give me strength.

"SIN:THETICA."

"Oh yeah. Right. I got it. There's a guy I know over at the Cascades Club who handles all their Grid work. From what I understand he's a regular at VTI. He's called Kravitz. I'll get him to hail you on the Grid and you can take it from there."

"I owe you, Jacks."

"Nah, forget it. It ain't no big thing. Can I ask you though … why the interest in Baptiste's bedtime stories?"

That's a cute concept of it.

"I gotta go in and take someone down. Wanna know what I'm getting myself into is all."

He ponders the idea.

"That's far out, man. Far out. But hey, be careful. Best not end up like one of those SIN:THETICA junkies, man."

What?

"Junkies?"

"Yeah. That stuff is seriously addictive. There's junkies all over the place. To be honest, I think Kravitz is one of them, though he'll flat out deny it when pushed."

This just keeps getting better and better.

"Addictive because they want to escape from their lives?"

"I'm not sure. Could be that silver shit they put into your eyes, I don't know. Whatever the case, it's made a whole bunch of addicts over the years."

Well now, what d'ya know. Jean-François Baptiste … drug dealer extraordinaire.

"I'm only going in once, Jacks. That's quite enough for me."

"If I had a dollar for every time I've heard that one."

He looks to one side and smiles a little, just as there's a split second glitch in the transmission and I get the oddest sense of déjà vu. Looking down now he types something, tells me he's hailed Kravitz, and then collapses the link.

That went a tad weird at the end there.

The glitch triggers a thought about the frequency disruptor I picked up from Zheng Zhu, so while I'm waiting for Kravitz to get in touch, I may as well get to work on installing it. Back outside and working on the Grav there's a big part of me that wants to jump in and disappear for good. The only thing that really keeps me here is my tie to Antoyah and River-Mai. I guess I haunt the sprawl like a ghost in bitter homage to their memory, but unlike them, I'm only dead on the inside.

By the time I get the call from Kravitz the disruptor is all hooked up and tested on a few nearby sentinels, so now I'm taking his transmission via my bracelet in the bedroom. I'm gathering ammo and weapons as we speak.

"I was told to call you. I'm Sonny Kravitz. You've got questions about VTI I've been told," says the black guy eyeing me suspiciously as I get armed to the teeth.

"You a friend of Jacks?"

"Well, I know him. Not sure if anybody's got friends in this city."

"That's good enough for me. Yeah, apparently you're a SIN:THETICA guy and you know the drill when it comes to immersion. How about you fill me in on the specifics and I'll make it worth your while?"

"Sounds good. Anything for my fellow Americans, but erm … can I ask you a question before we get into this?"

"Fire away."

"Are you the guy they call The Reverend? Seems like you fit the description from what I know."

"Guilty as charged."

"Goddamn."

He ponders this a second. "How many men you killed?"

"I thought I was asking the questions."

"Yeah, I know, I know, but erm … I'd just like to know is all."

Seems a good move to give him what he wants and then we can get on with it.

"As a soldier, too many to count. As a bounty hunter, getting on for one hundred."

"Holy shit. You're the real deal Mr. Reverend, sir. Wait till I tell the guys at the club who I was talking to. They'll flip."

"Can we get on with this or do I have to come looking for you?"

He gulps a little and takes the hint.

"What happens when they put the drops in your eyes?"

"Well now, it's kinda strange first time. It's like someone pouring ice-cold liquor in 'em. It runs around behind your eyeballs and feels like worms slithering their way inside your head. Some folk can't handle it. They freak out and have to be restrained, then removed from the programme before they've even begun. It settles down after a few seconds, so if you can ride it out you'll be over the worst of it."

Sounds fucked up, but whatever.

"What happens after that?"

"This is where the fun begins. You wake in someplace familiar. That could be your home or a hotel you've used before, or whatever. If you go in during the day it'll be daytime on the other side too, or if it's night then the same. The point of entry will be your extraction point also, so make sure you're there when you have to be."

"How do I know when I have to be there?"

"You're on countdown from the moment you go in. All you have to do is think about your clock and blink at the same time. The timer will enter your vision in your right eye and automatically fade out once you've checked it. It's fucking cool the first time you do it. Hell, I still think it's cool."

Doesn't sound all that complicated.

"What's this I hear about addiction?"

He shifts a little and that's a giveaway.

"Well, I don't know anything about that. Sure, I've heard the stories, but for my money an addict is an addict, is an addict. Some folk are just built that way, and no matter what they do, they're gonna get hooked on something."

"We wouldn't be talking about you would we, Sonny?"

He adopts an incredulous look.

"No way, man. The brothers don't be falling for no white man's game, no sir."

Which means the exact polar opposite.

"So, these 'stories' you've heard, as we're clearly not talking about you, what can you tell me?"

"They say the CTs can cause withdrawal. And I guess if your experience has been a positive one then the high you feel can lead to what feels like a crash when you come out. I don't know the tech stuff, but I suppose if someone's real unhappy in life then SIN:THETICA is sure gonna feel like a big-ass drug."

And this information not long after I had my moment this morning. Swell. I guess the emotional black hole that is me is all wired in the wrong direction for a trip like this, but screw it, a one-time deal surely can't be all that of a problem.

"Anything else I should know?"

He mulls it over briefly and then gives a quick shake of the head.

"Nah. That pretty much covers it, man."

"You've helped me stock up on a different kind of ammunition. I've got your token data. I'll wire what I think your advice was worth."

He goes to say something but I collapse the link. It's time to pack a few things and put the call in to Baptiste for a very different trip.

Despite what I've learned I still have an uneasy feeling. There's something telling me I'm still being outflanked by

Vargas, but I'll be damned if I know just how exactly. As I found out in the military, you never truly know your enemy until you step into the arena, and this is a big step for a lone wolf like me. I'll travel light for this one, and only take my Magnum and a couple of blades with me, as they'll be surrendered inside of VTI anyway. With a few things in a bag, I set my safe zone for lockdown for while I'm gone, and then hail SIN:THETICA's architect.

"Baptiste … I'm accepting your invite. What time at reception?"

"Ah, Mr. Hendrix, I had a feeling you'd take up my offer. You don't strike me as a man who easily backs down from a challenge. I'll inform my staff of your imminent arrival. Shall we say … 3.30? That way we can go through the contractual agreement and then get you prepared for immersion, post briefing. That should set you up for an early evening start time. I trust that meets with your approval?"

I simply nod, and then kill the feed.

Hell … I hate all this.

Chromium Contacts

My second visit to VTI is a very different affair. Security's cordial and Baptiste is waiting for me personally at the docking bay. Someone's got to take my Grav to the parking lot and I don't like that idea one bit. There's black market tech all over it and I don't want some trance factory grunt poking their nose into my setup. It's protocol, apparently, and relenting I tell the guy assigned to the job I'll know if he's tampered with anything.

Baptiste smiles a little, and tells me I'm one of a kind as we head on in. The induction is just pure boredom and lasts for what seems like forever. There's about three pieces of vital information I need to know in a sea of asinine explanatory notes, and I endure a medical wherein the young doctor can't help but marvel at my battlefield reassembly.

Can we just get to the starting line with this?

After granting consent, I'm taken to a private holding room where I strip and stow my belongings, before putting on something akin to a hospital gown and being led to my designated booth. Baptiste shadows me all the way and I'm not sure whether that's out of hospitality or a morbid fascination with my unease. The waiting technician puts me on a drip and Baptiste talks me through each sensor placement as they're attached all over.

The chair is comfortable enough—in fact it's probably the most comfortable thing I've ever sat on, given the fact it moulds to my frame and has me suspended at about 30°. I'm asked to insert my arms into its restraints: this being a necessary procedure for the application of the CTs. The thing Kravitz described as worms crawling behind your eyes is only minutes away, and I'm a little skittish now that the moment is upon me.

Baptiste leans in and smiles broadly.

"Are you ready for the experience of a lifetime, Mr. Hendrix?"

"Not really, but I'm going in anyway."

He puts a hand on my shoulder and whispers into my ear. "You're in safe hands, Balaam. Your welfare is our number one priority."

There's that sense of déjà vu again.

His distraction allows the tensioning of the restraints to go momentarily unnoticed, and when I've realised I can feel my pulse is up. There's no way I can get off this chair if I decide I want to, so we're passed the point of no return.

"We could do with getting your heart rate down, Mr. Hendrix. Please take some deep breaths to steady your nerves," offers the technician monitoring my stats.

I do as asked, as Baptiste eyes me like I'm some kind of VTI trophy specimen. I forget that someone in my line of work will be a rare bird in this circus.

"We can always introduce a sedative if you're feeling anxious," Baptiste offers.

It's like it's a test or something, to see if I'll cave in. I'm already tired of his games and I haven't even gone under yet. There's just that look I give, and he grins a little, doubtless thinking I'm playing along when all I want to do is punch his face in.

"Let's just cut the crap and get on with it."

The technician turns away and picks up a bottle of the Chromium Teardrops. There's a fleeting return in my mind to those mock torture sessions they had us endure in our Corps days: designed to make us almost unbreakable should we fall into enemy hands. Baptiste leans in and looms over me.

"It's like a ride on the Bullet-Tram. Only faster, and without any safety features," he imparts with a grin.

The first drop out of the pipette makes contact with my left eye and I blink from pure reflex, before the second hits the other and there's just nothing in the way of a reaction. The technician puts my visor on, and after a few seconds there's still nothing to speak of.

So much for Baptiste's wild boast.

And then …

I can safely say I've never seen a room melt before. It's like something colossal just pinched the scene between its massive fingers, and everything's rushing into that constricted point. As Kravitz said, I'm thrashing against what seems an invasion of worms sliding around my eyes into the cavities they occupy, and though all I see is light and imagery collapsing, I know my back is arched off the chair as I lock up in primal response.

It's ripping at me for seconds that seem an eternity, and then I fall. A calm, tranquil fall, before it picks up speed and the adrenaline builds to almost overload as I descend through endless dark. All of my senses are aching now and this must be what dying is like. I'm letting go. Can't hold on any longer … The other side greets me with the sights, sounds, and smells of NeuTokyo. It's cold as I step from an alley onto the broadway. Having something solid underfoot feels odd, and I draw my coat around me as I get my bearings.

Fuck, it's as real as anything I've known. Where am I? What part of the city have I been dropped into? Litter swirls on the breeze, and I lift my collar before blowing into my hands for what little warmth I can get. A distant rumble of thunder is the first thing that speaks to me and I don't like its tone one bit. When the wind drops the rain will follow and I'd rather be inside someplace when it does. A glance around tells me I'm probably in the old industrial zone. Factories converted into apartments dominate a scene interspersed with seedy joints and street dealers. There's a muted atmosphere here and I smirk as I remove an old-fashioned paper flyer that wraps around my calf, having drifted airborne across my path.

It reads: The Lord hath forsaken thee. For thou art but a lamb lost in the Devil's Playground. Seek salvation in the Soul Syndicate, whose shepherds will guide you back to green pastures.

There's a picture of a lamb inside a pentagram and details of where they can be contacted. I crumple it in my palm, and go to toss it just as some small inkling somewhere stays my hand. I unfold it, and JT's talk of sanctuary is now all too clear. I don't believe in any of this voodoo bullshit, but instead of this sheet of 'old-time religion' getting thrown away it finds itself inserted into the inside pocket of my all-weather coat.

Hell, I know I'm on a mission, but my curiosity is just a bitch right now. I'm standing here wondering if booze is just as real as everything else I see and feel around me. There's a spot across the broadway called *The Sunken Windjammer*, with patrons spilling onto wide steps out front. Its nautical theme tells me its owner is probably an ex-river rat, and likely someone well connected to the district's black market activities. Seems I can satisfy my curiosity on one score and maybe come out with some intel into the bargain. Crossing the street, I'm scoped immediately by those now trading whispers on my approach. None of them look heavyweight and they part like the civilian small fry they are, as I ascend into the lobby of this sleazy dive.

The music is some fucked-up fusion of Asian old school and a burnt out tenth generation resurrection of some guitar-driven noise. I must be old, because whatever I'm supposed to 'get' about it is totally lost on me. It just sounds a backdrop of mental ward exercise hour, coupled with some wailing Oriental dame who sounds like she's lamenting the horror of her wardrobe malfunction. The majority of the drinkers here are way younger than me and I can see that 'holy fuck' thought process as I drift through in search of the owner's corner these places tend to have. They can read my aura, and even drunk get the idea they'll be way out of their depth if they step out of line. Like most bars it's on a number of levels, and the light is all strobe and laser, with an atmosphere thick with sweat, smoke and whatever's emanating from those dark corners. I follow my instincts, and sure enough, it isn't long before two goons think they're going to bar my way to their employer.

"We don't know your face, and Mr. DeSantos doesn't do business with strangers," says the wide, bald grunt to my right.

His counterpart has his hand on the grip of a handgun inside his long coat, and beams like it makes him the alpha hard-on in the room.

It strikes me that even in VR I can't get away from these types of dicks.

Out comes a No-Glo and I spark it up, ignoring their brick wall tactics and posturing.

"Well, you tell Mr. DeSantos I've come about the damage to his property he ain't too happy about."

They share a confused look before the penny drops and the posturing gets amplified.

"You'd better haul ass, sugar … or things will get ugly, real quick," gun-boy prompts.

Now I know I can die inside this construct by all accounts, but what happens to these two? I mean, are they figments of my imagination or what? I've no idea how this really works but I'm guessing I might find out sooner, rather than later.

"I'm not going anywhere, but 'you' are. You're going to tell your boss The Reverend is doing house calls, and if he finds the hospitality of this place lacking, he's gonna be delivering some righteous retribution, starting right here with 'the twins of dumb-fuckery'."

It seems to have the desired effect, as gun-boy takes his hand off the piece and fat man drains of colour at the mention of my moniker. The pair are confused, seemingly unsure how to respond and whether moving even an inch is a good idea or not.

"So far you've called me 'sugar', threatened me, and not offered me a drink, so it's fair to say the DeSantos place is looking way down on my shit list."

Call it instinct, or call it whatever the fuck you want, but I'm suddenly aware of the meatheads behind me. Ducking, a fist clips the rim of my hat and sends it flying behind the bar. On the spin, I let blaze and the whole place lights up. My assailant gets a bullet and dead space where half of his head used to be while gun-boy, now behind me, picks up the entire blade depth of the throwing knife I've let loose by stopping it with his throat. Some hand cannons take out sections of the bar to my right, as the goons discharging them couldn't hit me if I stood still and drew a target on my chest.

It's all muzzle flares and screams, and the stampede of drinkers moves disjointed in the strobe light. In a rush there's three of them on me, and out goes the first as the knuckleduster guard on the handle of my Magnum-Drive puts a crack right through his jaw. I flip the second as he grabs my arm and his face connects with the brass bar rail, which frees me up to bury four rounds into asshole number three. He comes apart like shit through a meat grinder, and all the while fat man looks on in frozen trauma. I put my gun to his forehead and issue the most important instruction he's going to get all year.

"Go get my fucking hat."

***

My hat's now back where it belongs and DeSantos sits opposite with his hands where I can see them. The fat man is busy pouring me that drink I was initially denied. His hand is a little shaky, so I tell him to pour himself one too and sit his big ass down. His boss is the usual greasy fuck; all name brand cologne, cigar, and tacky gold bling. He twitches every now and again; just an eye thing which betrays his nerves. My own cigar got flattened underfoot in the waste of good ammo they put me through, so I light another, put my feet up on the table edge and lean back in my chair. Vaguely wagging my gun in DeSantos's direction, I press 'The King of Nowhere' about the Shepherds of the Almighty.

"What dealings do you have with the Soul Syndicate?"

There's a slight pause in his whole manner, like he's pondering a lie, before he pipes up.

"They move stuff for me. Designer drugs, sometimes arms."

Why the pause? Why the lie?

"Given what I know about that shady outfit, you've just told me the obvious. Human trafficking has always been the crux of their operation. I'm betting you're up to your eyeballs in the stink of it, DeSantos, and truth be known, I don't give a rat's ass because I'm not here to blow your little arrangement wide open. What I want is your contact. Tell me who that is, and where I can find them, and I'll turn a blind eye to the shit you're pulling. If not, I'll make it my business to run you 'out of business' and I'll start with this place tonight. The Windjammer will be sunk for real and I'll make her skipper watch her burn in the harbour, so to speak."

He takes what I perceive to be a resigned draw on his cigar, exhales the smoke, and sighs.

"Are you going to make them bleed?" he asks.

"It's not my intent. I'm looking for somebody and I think they'll know where I might find him."

"What makes you think that?"

"Because this particular sheep is a Vargas sheep, which gives him a golden fleece in a flock of the ordinary."

Mention of Vargas seems to rattle him a tad.

This drink is going down real easy and oh yeah, part of the reason I came in here in the first place: yep, booze does taste exactly like the real thing.

"My contact is a guy called Primo, but it's not like I can just call him outside of our standard arrangements. If it isn't about business I can pretty much guarantee he'll just hang up on me," DeSantos opines.

It's my turn to take that long draw on a cigar.

"Then tell him some asshole came in and shot up the place. Came in asking about your operation after taking out your hired muscle. Then say he's gonna come back in a few hours wanting a face-to-face with your connection. That should slap his bitch ego hard and he'll come armed to the teeth with an entourage."

"You've got this all figured out haven't you."

"That's why I'm still sucking air and your goons are making a mess of the captain's quarters here."

Having glanced at the bodies, I reach down and retrieve my blade from gun-boy's throat. DeSantos brings up a holo-page from that chunk of gold on his wrist and hails his black market contact. He rattles off pretty much what I told him, word for word, and Primo does all the posturing I expected him to do. He'll be here in half an hour.

"Where's the back office and the sub-system you use for your operation?" I ask.

DeSantos indicates over his shoulder.

"Lead the way, fat man," I say, with a wag of the Magnum-Drive.

When we get to the hub of operations, I tell DeSantos to get his ass in his office chair, after I remove the two pieces of military hardware he's got stashed beneath the desk. Throwing one to the fat man, I eject the rounds from the other and toss it. Exchanging glances, the two of them look confused before I clarify the situation.

"You're gonna be my back-up man," I say, pointing to the big guy.

He looks even more confused than he has been so far and I'm guessing DeSantos can't believe he's not emptied a clip into me by now. Thing is, he's seen me waste his crew and knows he's minor league when it comes to the grown-up stuff.

"You just stand there and look like you intend to use that thing. Shouldn't be too difficult for an actress of your pedigree," I instruct him.

DeSantos shakes his head in disbelief.

"If you ain't dead by the time this is over, you're fired," he informs him.

In the time it takes Primo and his 'cheerleaders' to turn up, I to and fro with DeSantos about his stake in the game and the amount of money he's taking. Seems with everything he's wrapped up in, he's worth a cool chunk of change, a sprawling pad on the north side and a luxury yacht anchored at a marina in the bay. I should have been a career criminal instead of the guy who mops up their constant mess.

What they do filters through everything and nine times out of ten I'm hunting down someone associated with their food chain to some degree. I'm just a fucking garbage man really. Even in this high-tech simulation I'm still shovelling shit. The hum of the arriving Gravs kills our conversation and fat man's starting to look more than a little nervous.

There's the clatter of the old-fashioned elevator that's bringing them down from the aero-pad and it's a final ten seconds which gives me the time I need to ready weapons. I stand behind DeSantos to, in part, use him as a shield but also to keep my gun aimed squarely at his back. He knows exactly why I'm stood behind and it's going to dictate every move he makes in his dealings with Primo.

The docking noise makes fat man jump slightly and I stifle a grin as the doors part to reveal the man who's going to feed me my own testicles, apparently. He's a thin, arrogant-looking specimen; kinda reminds me of Vargas, ironically—all slicked back hair and reptile features. He's flanked by four gorillas who've brought enough firepower to bury me a hundred times over.

"Greetings to the man who's going to beg me for his life in under an hour from now."

Primo's entrance and statement remind me why I couldn't actually be a career criminal: I simply couldn't pull off the sense of pantomime they all seem to adhere to without laughing myself out of the city limits. He walks the floor, with mob in tow, and stops about six feet away from the desk. The tacky leather gloves come off in overly dramatic fashion, before the overcoat he's sporting, with both being tossed onto a low cabinet sat in the gloom.

What a performance. He's a natural at this kind of thing. Me? I just kill people and don't bother with the theatrics.

His admirers level their guns at me with equal flair, due to the over-emphasised cocking of their mechanics. There's a few seconds of this 'entertaining charade' left hanging there; long enough for it to, I suppose, look intimidating, before Primo unleashes his next assault of verbal diarrhoea.

"It troubles me deeply that you can't take care of your own affairs, DeSantos. When we're through with the 'Culpepper Cowboy' here, you're going to get some re-education of your own."

I'll admit, there was at least some wit in that delivery, but I'm bored already and that's where any stand-up comedy routine is going to just fall flat for me. A round from a Magnum-Drive will down anything on the planet—that's just a fact. Rounds from a modified one will take that scenario into a whole different realm, as was the case when Ganz got decapitated.

Four shots in quick succession see Primo standing there with his crisp, expensive threads dowsed in blood, and DeSantos' bullet-ridden torso detached from the rest of him, and laid out as a dismembered mess across the desk. Why bother to shoot around the Windjammer's patron, when him being there poses no problem for an upgraded weapon? Besides, he'd served his purpose, so I no longer need him.

It's funny when a pumped up prick suddenly gets separated from his protection. I march across the bloody floor and get the fucker by the throat.

"Come here you little weasel."

I drag him to that cabinet he dropped his coat and gloves on, and I kick his legs out from under him.

"Oh, I'm sorry, did that hurt?"

As soon as he's seated, I connect my gun's knuckleduster guard with the bridge of his nose, and it gives as I'd expect it to. Now he's wearing his own blood too, and that searing pain only a broken nose can bring is lancing *through* his head. *Got the answer you wanted, big shot?* While he's busy with his streaming extremity, I find a chair and put it opposite, and sit my ass down in front of him. Fat man seems to have disappeared and in all the excitement I didn't clock his exit. Shame, as we were getting along famously.

"It's not a great feeling is it?"

He looks up and shakes his head a little.

"Here, use this," I say, handing him one of his highly priced gloves and thereby adding insult to injury.

You can see he's torn. He needs to try and stem the flow but he knows how much he paid for them. Oh, it gives me a warm, fuzzy feeling inside.

"Here's the thing. I've seen just about every act under the sun. And yours … how can I put it? Well, it's a well-worn routine I've seen hundreds of times before. So, here's the deal. I'm going to try my best to forget the fact I didn't find you very entertaining at all, and you're going to tell me everything I want to know. If not, well then I'm going to have to use the five-star rating system on you."

Through the look of pain there's a moment of confusion, so I clarify for him.

"Despite your thoroughly unimaginative performance, I'm prepared to give you a glowing five-out-of-five review. You get the first star when I blow your right foot off. The second when the left comes off. Then you get the third and fourth when your hands get separated, and finally you get the fifth when I blow your balls off and put them in your boring mouth. How does that sound? After all, I'm known for my impartiality and fairness."

He doesn't say a thing, and merely nods in silent agreement. Now there's a performance I 'can' appreciate.

***

Even in spite of all the unnecessary theatrics, I did enjoy my subsequent chat with Primo. I found him to be cordial and compliant, and not even in the least bit whiney when I levelled my gun at his temple and added his exploding head to the bloodbath. Credit where credit is due, he didn't even flinch or cry like a bitch when karma caught up with him. Just goes to show, someone's final performance can indeed be their best.

Back on the streets and armed with an address for a Soul Syndicate bolthole, thinking about Primo's arrival makes me wonder whether I have access to my Grav in this setup. I have everything else, so it stands to reason I should have my ride too. I click the button on my location transponder and, sure enough, it's just a few blocks away—right around the corner from where VTI dropped me in. I remember Kravitz talking about the timer you're supposed to be able to access and take a moment to try and concentrate to bring it up. Nothing happens at first and so I'm guessing I'm probably doing it wrong, but then a faint image makes its way into my vision and reveals I've spent about two hours in immersion so far. I'll take that, as it's not long in the scheme of things and I've got a lead to pursue.

Inside the Chrysler, I feed in the address Primo tapped into my bracelet. As I sync the devices, I recognise the location. The city plan scrolls across the holo-screen and continues its sweep before locking down on an apartment one block away from my own. Seems kind of odd. But then again, these creepy bastards have property all over the city, so…Traffic is strangely low-key en route and as I buzz over my own building, I notice the lights are on in my safe zone.

What the fuck? But it dawns on me I'm in Baptiste's construct, so it doesn't necessarily mean a thing. Still, it's got me wondering, and even as I land I can't help thinking there's something to it. I'll be heading there when I'm done here. I kill the drivetrain, and put the Grav in defence mode, before punching in the access code on the bolthole's security panel, which Primo kindly voiced before his head took a permanent vacation from his body.

Piece in hand, I walk the corridor as the lights come on low and I take my first real draw on the odours in here. There's incense of some kind, and drug vapour residue, and the trace of body odour in the mix. I'm guessing this place hasn't been aired in a while. A hum is coming from behind the door straight in front me. Something is in constant use but I can't discern what it is. There's zero movement in the entire space but that don't mean shit. Primo said there was a syndicate brother here who knew exactly where I'd find my man Treece.

Sure, even under the notion I'd let him go, Primo could've offered up a bum steer, but something told me he believed the lie and so I'm not expecting this tip-off to be a dud. Whether the guy is here now is another matter. If he is, the last thing I want is a firefight, because if I waste him I'm back to square one. I'm going to do what I never do. I'm going to ditch the stealth approach and let it be known I'm here for talks, not aggression.

"Hey, Primo said you're the man I need to see."

I keep my gun trained on the door where the noise is coming from. There's no answer.

Did that fucker send me into a trap? Is the room full of goons armed to the teeth?

I inch further inside and instinct tells me to ignore other doors and focus on the one ahead. Getting closer, it suddenly feels cold in here—damp almost. It's something which doesn't seem to correlate with the overall impression of the building and its inner space. If anything, it appears well-maintained and this corner of the city is a decent neighbourhood. I'm at a point where I can see traces of my breath but there's no feel of cold, outside air coming in from an open window somewhere. If I didn't know any better, I'd swear I was immersed in water. As fast as it invades my awareness, it's gone again and leaves me shivering from a strange sensation as opposed to actually being cold.

What was that all about?

I'm just feet from the door now and the hum is louder. I still can't figure out what's making the noise but there's no let-up in its output. If I step any closer to the door it will auto-open, so without any response from the tenant, it's looking like I'm going to have to bite the bullet and make the first move. I pull a spare ammo clip from inside my coat, hunker down, and slide the magazine across the floor towards it. The motion sensor above picks it up and I figure if he lets off a round or two, then I'm below the chest height he'll probably go for. All I'm greeted with when the door slides open is a burst of more light and the continual hiss of white noise. I stay low for a few seconds in case he makes a move, and then slowly rise and cock my head to get a better view inside.

Now at the threshold, I see a large living space and the two things which immediately grab my attention are the huge holo-screen which is the source of the noise, and a high-tech scope sitting on a tripod at the far end of the room. There's drug-taking paraphernalia on the low table but no immediate threat in the form of an occupant. I retrieve the ammo clip and enter. The entertainment hub has the volume set on maximum, and the static white display it's synced to, is casting long shadows throughout. I find the power source and kill it, but there's no total loss of light as the room's residuals came on when I stepped in. Thank fuck the noise has stopped. There's not much out of the ordinary here but that scope's got me intrigued. I'm guessing 'Syndicate Sam' has himself some voyeuristic tendencies.

But, before I go and check it out, I'd best make sure the rest of the pad is empty too. About five minutes is what it takes to check the rest of the rooms and be satisfied no one's home. Now for that scope. It's a pretty high-tech piece of hardware with a handsome mode selection and excellent range. I cock my hat and set my eye to it. It needs adjusting to my sight and that's done by a neat little feature which scans my orb and makes the necessary fine tuning.

Hell, I can see the detail right through that window over there and …

Someone's playing fucking games. I doubt what I'm seeing for a second, but it's only self-preservation kicking in. Why the fucking hell has this motherfucker got eyes on my apartment? And yeah, the lights are still on and the external armoured shutters are on lock-back. I pull away from the eyepiece. Shit, that means someone either has access to, or has overridden, the security features.

My concern is real enough, but the scenario isn't, and I just have to keep reminding myself that all of this is make-believe, or something. It's pretty damn hard, as everything is totally life-like in every way. I struggled with that just now. In the short amount of time I've been in this I seem to have taken several steps away from one reality to another. *What was it Jacks said? Oh yeah, SIN:THETICA junkies.* I gotta stay mindful of that. It's easy to see how someone could lose their grip on the everyday doing too much of this. Just to satisfy a strange urge I get, I take another eye-spy through the looking glass and see the shadow of someone moving around the place. To figure someone is there and to actually see a trace of it are two different things altogether. It just trips my trigger and I'm spinning on my heel out of here.

Something which went unnoticed on the floor gets kicked from my path in my haste and the detective in me just can't let it slide. I have to haul up and satisfy my curiosity. Ah, hell, it's just a fucking book and unimportant… wait a minute. Picking it up I feel something rattle around inside. It's old, very old and a battered, dusty copy of *The Master Key: An Electrical Fairy Tale* by L. … Frank … Baum. Oh, just fuck-off—I swear Baptiste is screwing with my head.

This was the very thing I found in Treece's apartment which led me to VTI and down this rabbit hole in the first place. Flicking it open, I see the vast majority of its pages have been doctored with a square cut out to create a recess within. There's only more drugs paraphernalia inside, but the kicker is where that recess begins: page 57.

Is this thing a bible for these monkeys? Is there a hidden code in this I'm not seeing? One thing's for sure, I can't afford to ignore this as there's no way it's a coincidence. I set it down on the low table with the rest of the mind bleach tools and make for the front door. I'm going to take the elevator down and run the block on foot, because if I take the Grav I'll alert whoever's busy rolling my place as I set it down on the aero-pad. The streets are busy with the familiar sights and sounds, and the neon sheen of the intersecting drags is given a further luminescence by the rain which has just begun to fall. Rain in NeuTokyo; no shit. Seems VTI have even got that detail right. I lift my collar and tip my hat forward, and use the shadowy overhangs for cover as I head around the block.

On the strip outside my apartment, I cross over the broadway to get a visual on it. At street level, all I can see is the light spilling out and certainly no shadow like I saw earlier. I cross back over and head for the lobby. The rain hasn't cleared the street of human traffic, and I doubt that even if there's a lookout posted on the front steps, they'll get eyes on me in this stream of bodies, before I'm on top of them.

My palm acquires a blade as I close in, just as the beam from a single headlight flares beside the entrance, and a lone Aeroquad powers up and makes the jump from ground level into the flow of mechanised traffic above. I can't say for sure, but it's almost like that cycle and rider had the look of one of JT's crew. The downpour intensifies as I reach the main doors and the lobby overheads are flickering. If there's some muscle in a shady corner in there then they'll definitely have the edge on me.

I can't stand here all night. I go in with a roll and expect the inevitable gunshot. It doesn't come so I rise and do a quick three-sixty: no one. I bring the elevator down and roll in something from my coat's inner pocket. I set the carriage speed to slow and it begins its laboured ascent to my floor. I take to the stairs. It takes about a minute for it to rise and dock, and as the doors open the fucker I expected to be there gets knocked off his feet. I emerge from the stairwell to see him sprawled across the corridor, having taken a face-full of the stun grenade I sent up.

He's the floor watcher the rest of the fuckers inside my safe zone placed there as a buffer between me and them. I step over him and make for the door. I've replaced the blade I was carrying with the Magnum-Drive and I know, having heard the grenade, they're in position and waiting for my entrance.

Like my Grav, my apartment is full of black market tech, and between the two it's like having an armed unit of men to protect this old soldier. I whisper into my bracelet and a holo-page springs up which shows the inner hallway courtesy of the hidden camera I've got placed there. I see goon number two to the left of the main door and a third guy in hood and shades at the far end. Both have guns pointing at the door. I keep the image up long enough to satisfy myself that there's no one else inside, then collapse it.

I whisper another instruction into the wrist adornment and activate the main door override. Its hydraulics kick in and the expected rounds sail down the outer corridor. I'm out of sight, and I use the time and tension the standoff is creating to swap out my gun clip. The replacement's carrying scatter-heads and I figure that if I aim a few at the door's metal housing on the right, there's a good chance a fragment or two from the separating clusters will catch the deadbeat just beyond via ricochet.

I pump two at it, and then a third for good measure, and I'm sure I hear a groan just before a droning noise spills through the open door and drowns it out. It sounds like a Grav approaching and I realise it's either their back-up arriving at my aero-pad or the getaway they've called for. Swapping out my clips again, I get ready to run for the door. Elevator guy moans on the floor behind me but he'll be disorientated for a good while yet, so I concentrate solely on what's in front of me. I've got two choices: sit tight and use the fact they've got the narrow channel of a single door to emerge from, or get in there, take out number three and lock the place down against the extra muscle that's arriving. I'm through the door before I really weigh it up; probably because I'm pissed they're here in the first place.

Number two is sitting against the wall clutching his neck. There's blood seeping between his fingers and he's got that wide-eyed look you get when you're in the sub-minute slide towards checking out. His gun is by his side but there's no danger he's gonna use it on me. Hooded man is nowhere to be seen. I run and dive into the day room. He gets two shots off before I land behind the low-level open plan divider and he backs out through the door at the top of the steps leading to the aero-pad.

The room's been tossed; there's stuff everywhere. The Grav's shifting into lift-off outside so if there's extra muscle then they're still on board. I close the distance and race the stairs. I kick the door open and watch the over-sized transporter carry the grinning asshole away from harm. In the open cargo bay, he drops his hood, removes the shades, and gives me a mock salute as he's taken out of range: the very same errand boy Vargas sent here on day one of this total mindfuck.

Cyber Dirt's Just as Dirty

Cuffed and no doubt feeling the worst for wear, 'elevator stun grenade man' sits across the table from me. I've secured my place, so now it's just me and him, and I'm going to get answers if I have to pump him full of painkillers to keep the interrogation machine rolling. I pour myself some rum and spark a cigar. It's going to be a long session and it's been a while since I drubbed the merry fuck out of someone.

I start the questioning. "Word has it your boss takes people's heads off so at least you can be thankful before I begin I'm not that much of a psychopath."

He lifts his head and leans back in the chair.

"He's not my boss," he says, grinning.

I rub my jaw, and put on my best non-believer face.

"Vargas ain't your boss but you're just hanging with his associates for kicks, right?"

He shrugs.

I get up, move around the table, and with sleeves rolled up, I give him a solid punch to the jaw. There's blood, and a few teeth, which he deposits on the tabletop with a hooded glint in the eyes from that hanging head of his. He gives his best defiant laugh. I take a mouthful of booze and a draw on the No-Glo.

"The average adult has thirty-two teeth, generally speaking. We're not even half a minute into this escapade and you're down to thirty. Now, I'll admit, I've never been much of a mathematician but that looks like a pretty piss-poor ratio from where I'm standing."

He lifts his head a little and out pops the defiance I'm going to smash out of him.

"Fuck you."

He splices a bloody grin between gasps.

"Vargas is your boss," he hisses.

I blow out smoke and hammer him one more time. Out comes another of those upper front tombstones, which drops to the floor ahead of the slick of red that falls after. His mouth is starting to look too well ventilated.

"I make that 29, 'Cochise' … at this rate I'll have a new necklace by the time I've drained this here liquor bottle."

I pour another and take my seat again.

"I'm a Soul Syndicate acolyte. I told you, I don't work for Vargas," he manages to say.

"Then you'll know Primo. He's dead by the way. One less shepherd to gather the flock."

He doesn't react.

"If you're not a Vargas cockroach, then why are you shadowing his crew?"

"Got a smoke?" he asks.

"Sure."

I spark another of my cigars, reach across the table and put it in his mouth. He takes a draw and I watch its steadying effect take hold. I think I've got his cooperation now, but if not, I'll press on with the strong-arm tactics.

"Vargas bought our services. Brought us in for a special op," he says.

"Really? And what might that be?"

"To help you find your mark."

"Bullshit."

He tilts his head a little, takes another draw and exhales the next line.

"You're after Treece, right?"

"That I am, but ransacking my apartment doesn't fit in with your story. And why would Vargas's errand boy take off if you're all here to help me? You're gonna have to do better than that my friend."

He takes another draw.

"Vargas thinks you're hiding something from him."

"Hiding what exactly?"

"I have no idea. I was standing guard, remember? Vargas's heavy, Maddox, knew what he was looking for. He was the one who trashed your place."

I take a long, hard look at it. Finish my drink and pour another.

"And the biker outside?"

He gives what I take to be a genuine look of confusion.

"You've lost me, bounty hunter."

Instinct tells me he knows more than he's prepared to give at this point. I don't think he knows about the biker, but he's in need of a little more persuasion on everything else. I smile and reach for my gun. It's time to ramp up the damage.

"Primo gave me the answers I wanted and then I killed him. I'll cut you a deal. Give me the rest of it and I won't waste you."

The gun gets levelled at his chest.

"I'm not even going to count. None of that theatrical bullshit. I'm just going to get bored and even more angry when you don't comply, and then I'm going to put a cavernous hole where your heart and lungs are."

He nods in recognition and makes his play.

"Then you won't find Treece. What name did Primo give you before you took him out?"

"Spader."

He gestures to the items beside me on the table, the things I took off him when he was downed in the corridor. One of them is his bracelet.

"Sync yours with that. It'll bring up my Grid ID," he prompts.

I'm sceptical, but it won't hurt to find out. It seems Spader, John C, just saved his own ass.

"Well, well, if it ain't a revelation from the good book itself. Seems we've got something in common, mister black market acolyte."

He squints, either because of query, pain, or both.

"We've been in each other's apartments," I clarify.

I rise, go get a towel, wet it, and return to drop it on the table in front of him. I uncuff his hands from the back of the chair but shackle one hand to the table leg.

"Use that to clean up your face," I say, pointing.

I go to get another cup from the kitchen, as I figure his head hammering deserves a slug of rum as compensation. Poured, it gets pushed in front of him.

"You're honoured. No one gets my booze."

I raise mine in salute and he gingerly takes a sip. That mouth of his is going to be raw for quite a spell and he'll have the headache from hell. I suddenly have a thought.

"How did Maddox override my security?"

He frowns, as if the answer isn't obvious.

"He had your pass codes and a retinal simulacrum."

I almost choke on my rum.

What the fuck? Only my encrypted Grid vault has the former and my medical files the latter. It would take a software genius to crack those and …

Baptiste. The only brain that fits the bill.

I'm just staring at Spader. He's probably wondering if I'm going to make good on that threat to blow his lungs out. I'm drifting. My thought process is fried from what I can't compute. Then another thought kicks in.

"What's with the book in your apartment?"

He thinks for a second.

"It's just a throwback to bygone days. I read somewhere on the Grid that users used to stash their supply and kit in chopped-out books. Back in the day when it was outlawed and their pads would get raided. It's just a nod to that."

Oh yeah, it's just a nod to that.

"It's the same book I found in Treece's apartment. Both copies with a focus on page 57. Strikes me as very odd. Too much of a coincidence, if you will. Stop me when you want to jump in and rattle off some more bullshit."

* * *

Spader's reluctance to squeal had forced me to get all nasty again. Sitting now with that towel I'd given him, he's doing another mop-up job on that face of his. Turns out Vargas had given him that book. Not having any specific instructions on what to do with it, he'd turned it into his drugs stash. Clearly, Vargas is fucking with me. But to what end? I'd not come across Spader on the outside, yet here he was in this construct. Which, if I've got what Baptiste told me as correct, means he's also at VTI, in a booth and immersed like me. Either that, or his association with Vargas has been uploaded into this simulation. My head is totally fucked with all of this. All I can do for now is focus on finding Treece and just let the rest play out the way it's gonna.

"So where can I find Treece?"

He looks up and sighs. "Other side of the city. We have safe houses everywhere. I know where we had him last, but moving flesh is our trade. We don't keep anyone in one place for very long. He might still be there, he might not."

"Wait a minute. Let's just back this thing up a tad. This whole deal has me totally confused. So Treece goes to VTI to get away from Vargas. Runs to the Soul Syndicate through immersion, and now you're telling me the syndicate is gonna let me have him on a plate as they've cut a deal with Vargas? It just doesn't stack up. If that's the case, what the fuck am I involved for? You could just deliver him yourselves."

He frowns as if I'm stupid or something. "Because he's here but he ain't. He's really at VTI. Besides, Vargas only cut a deal with some of us in the syndicate. There's lots of others who know nothing about the arrangement. As far as they're concerned they're figuring out a way to get Treece—the real Treece—out of VTI, so that he has real 'flesh trade' value to cut a deal with Vargas. Yeah, I know, I can tell by that look on your face we're just rats, fucking each other over for the money."

It still doesn't add up.

"If Vargas has cut a deal with some of you, and you have access to Treece, then why does he need me?"

He shrugs.

"All I know is we get a pay-off if you get to find him. That's it, man. I don't have anything else. We get our money and our bosses are none the wiser."

"Unless Vargas gets what he wants and then informs your bosses of your disloyalty, in order to curry favour with them and not have to pay you a single dollar. Because of course, you'll be dead," I point out.

He takes a deep breath and lives his little 'oh fuck' moment, before deflecting it back at me.

"Sure, those are the risks. And if that applies to me, then it applies to you too. If Vargas wants you to get him, but you can't extract him, I don't see how you can do what he wants. He won't like that. The way I see it, it doesn't matter where the fuck he's hiding in this construct, all that matters is where he's at inside the VTI building. If you catch up with him in here, there's no way he's gonna give you that information, even if you try to beat it out of him."

Of course he's right, and it's not like I can kill Treece's other self in here. It's not what Vargas wants. He wants 'cyber Treece' disposed of so he can have the comatose version plucked from VTI. The whole thing is just a complicated shitshow. I get the feeling now I'm not just missing 'something,' but 'everything.' The fact that none of this adds up tells me there's something else going on entirely, but I doubt if a complete nobody like Spader knows any of the truth either. So what's my options? I can't get out of immersion until my allotted time is up. I could just hit a bar and get tanked, or maybe go to a brothel. Or, I could just focus and do what I came into this ridiculous set-up to do in the first place: find Treece. It seems Vargas has put multiple irons in the fire in order to get his man. It shouldn't surprise me really, he's king rat in the city's sewer system.

"So I take it the syndicate are just sitting on the fact that Treece is in suspension until they orchestrate a way to bust him out of Baptiste's building?"

He nods.

"So Vargas is playing just about everyone he can in order to get this fucker, right?"

He nods again.

"I guess so," he adds.

I wonder how many other roaches are just gonna come skittering out of the cracks in the walls while I'm on Treece's trail?

"What's the address and pass codes of the place I need to go to?"

He spills what I need, so I uncuff him. At gunpoint, I have him take a little walk up the steps to the aero-pad and he gets to hesitating.

"Where are we going?" he asks.

"We're not going anywhere, but 'you' are."

"Hey man, you got your answers. What the fuck is this?"

"Ah, you think I'm going to off you," I say, laughing, and lying.

"Not today, Spader. You're gonna be my worm on a hook to catch a bigger fish."

I hand him his bracelet. "Hail Maddox."

"He'll come armed to the teeth and with an entourage," he predicts.

"That's exactly what I'm counting on."

If Vargas thinks I'm hiding something from him then I'm going to pull a move which will get his attention. It stands to reason that Maddox will just be itching to find out exactly what Spader has told me. He'll come heavy-handed, but I have an idea which just might swing the odds in my favour. I want these goons off my trail and I want Vargas to get the message I'm not to be fucked with. It's still raining outside, though not as heavy, and it's funny how it feels exactly the same. The city is full of noise and its usual array of odours, and just for a moment I marvel at the complexity of Baptiste's construct. Even with my hat and long coat back on I feel the moisture in the air. I feel immersed in it. It's not the first time I've felt that. Back at Spader's apartment I got a sense of the very same. I wonder if it's a quirk of the software?

Spader has requested pick-up, and so the carrier is only minutes away now. It hits me how I'm not craving any Narcoplex and I guess because I'm in suspension my nerve-endings aren't needing their usual fix. But I am thinking of that unfinished rum bottle back in my apartment, and can't wait to get this over with. Spader wants to talk now. Funny, I had to beat it out of him not that long ago. I tell him to shut up, just before I slam the butt of my Magnum-Drive into the base of his skull. He goes down fast and I turn him over face down to cuff his hands behind his back. Reaching into my coat, I retrieve a little piece of beauty and slip it into the rear pocket of his pants. It's only about a centimetre thick, and so it should go unnoticed at a cursory glance.

The lights from Spader's ride come into view and I watch the Grav's approach as it does a pass before coming about and making a calculated descent to the lip of the aero-pad. Vargas' lapdog grins all the way down, standing as he does in the open cargo bay surrounded by his cronies who are, as Spader predicted, armed to the teeth. The driver's got eyes on me too. He's probably waiting for me to spring some shit on them, so his drop is a tentative one. I slowly bring up the Magnum-Drive and point it square at their wheel-man. Maddox reads my intent and knows one false move means they lose their control over the craft and it's a big 'ole helter-skelter down to decorate the broadway below.

The Grav levels off a few feet over the edge and Maddox stays put. Two of his henchmen step off and take the few steps needed to lift the unconscious Spader off the pad. There's that same tension, just like when I had my first run-in with him when he showed up at my place back in the real world. It's a fighter thing. We both want that chance to square up and see who's the more brutal animal in the ring.

I keep my aim on the driver and they deposit Spader onto the cargo bay floor. I watch the fleeting look from Maddox to his hired muscle and read the moves you learn only as a soldier. I knew the moment I met him he was a pro and these exchanges are all the evidence I need to solidify that initial assessment. He even gives another mock salute as the transporter slips into gear for ascent.

I put my gun away and put a No-Glo in my mouth. I bring up the lighter and keep my eye on the grinning asshole who's mouthing a slow and obvious line amid the noise of the thrusters—*'on any other day.'* He laughs as the Grav gains height and I go to spark up my cigar with what looks like my lighter. Except it ain't, see. It's that remote unit I acquired from Zheng, which marries with those compact fragmentation plates I got a whole raft of recently—one of which is tucked away neatly in Spader's pocket. I thumb the button and smile as I watch Maddox drop his theatrics and turn inside the cab on hearing the three-second primer engage. There's the inevitable panic, and mad scramble, and Maddox looks back one last time to see me mouth the words—*'today's that fucking day.'*

The explosion punches sections of the Grav into a glittering arc and it's thrown into an instant spin. The initial flare gives way to trails of grey and black smoke as the shock wave, and what's left of the thrust assembly, propels it into a spiral descent. I walk to the ledge and watch as the burning metal wreck spills bodies on its way to total destruction, as it makes contact with the adjacent building roughly halfway to ground level.

The final explosion rips it in two, with a fireball that lights up the broadway in its scatter of fuel, flame, and fragments of everything that's left on board. Vargas just got his message and I've hopefully got a simpler task on my hands without his goons on my tail. They'll all be in a coma at VTI now and that deserves a celebration courtesy of that rum that's waiting for me.

***

They say a dog will only stand off from a foe it doesn't understand. It will tackle something many times its own size if it knows a thing will fight in the same instinctive manner. That's a lot of bravery in a compact creature. That's how the military make their own. In conflict, a soldier will only lay low if the enemy is an unknown quantity. I've had no time in real terms to find out anything about Treece. And, though he's not the enemy per se, he's the reason this whole clusterfuck is happening. Spader gave me a possible location, but as I take this moment to reflect on everything so far, I'm left with a sense of loss before I even acquire my mark. Vargas is the real animal I don't understand and yet I've willingly stepped into the arena with him. As the rum goes down I have to wonder if I'm celebrating or drowning my sorrows.

And then it hits me. That wave of misery I try to keep contained. You can't have emotions in my profession, but then you can't be human without them. Every person I waste I use as another stone to heap on the burial plot of my past. I kid myself the weight of each will keep the pain from welling up out of that hole in my soul. The liquor isn't going to be enough to suppress it, and so I use it to wash down the pill I've not needed thus far.

It won't make any difference, as it's for another kind of pain altogether, but in truth I'm a junkie and my brain wants its fix regardless. I'm in no mood to leave my apartment right now, so I bring up a holo-page from my bracelet and activate the remote pilot which will bring my Grav from Spader's aero-pad to mine. I gotta get myself pulled round because this is exactly the wrong time for a slide into the sombre to be happening.

I've got the shakes, and it's going to be a while before I'm in the right shape to press on. Knowing I shouldn't, but unable to stop myself, I use the bracelet to access my most secret files and bring up the only photograph I have of my girls. It's going to crush me but it's all I've got in this wretched space I call my life. I reach, as if touching the artificial will give me a sense of the real. It brings real tears. No, check that. Virtual ones in response to real emotion. I can't even get my head around that right now.

Their smiles echo the warm day that photograph was taken. God, I miss them both. Only in moments like this, is this dog vulnerable. I feel my face is streaked, like so many other times. Times when I could easily put the gun in my mouth and eat a bullet. A fragment of hope always tells me I'd be with them if I did, but the rest of me knows that thought is a cruel mistress.

I take a long slug of the rum and a deep draw on that cigar I lit on the way back inside. The sound of my Grav docking at the pad bleeds in through my haze of despair. It's a cold, metallic reminder of the need to keep moving forward, both in life and on this mission. I collapse the page and it snaps the image from my sight.

I've often told myself at least I have something to cling to. There are countless out there who have nothing. So I tell myself again and the shakes begin to ease down. The days of talking through my inner damage with endless shrinks will always haunt me. They'd claim they got me fixed eventually, but I remember those post-war years as nothing but a trail of wreckage I don't recall ever crawling out from. Sure, there was my jewel, Antoyah, but even she couldn't erase what the war had put upon me.

Therapy for Post Traumatic Stress Disorder. Counselling for assimilation back into society, and of course my meds to combat any deviation from the correct orientation in my thinking. I had it all. But whether or not it made any real difference I can't say. I function I suppose, so there's that, but a big part of me still feels like I'm face down on that battlefield, and I ain't ever leaving. They said those feelings would pass. They haven't. They said 'the noise' inside my skull would quieten down and go away. It hasn't. How many nights have I put my head down only to have the dark bring all of the horror back? I guess that's why I'm here. It takes a fucked-up someone to want to even entertain the idea of cutting a deal with Vargas.

I know I've never moved on from my loss. In every sense. I've never really wanted to let anyone in, ultimately because I knew I wouldn't be able to suffer anymore. Besides, once I became a hunter, I simply couldn't trust a living soul and that's why I'll be empty until I'm ash at the crematorium. There's a kind of safety in solitude anyway. When you put yourself at the mercy of others you're exposed, and it takes more mental ammunition than I've got to rescue that scenario. I pour another drink and watch a fly crawl across the refrigerator door. Shit … VTI have even factored for that in this triumph of cerebral mesmerism. I raise the glass in mock tribute and knock its contents back in one.

The fly's now airborne and comes to land on the table next to my liquor bottle. Drawn by the aroma I'm guessing. If that's true, then SIN:THETICA truly is a wonder. I watch it sample a rum drop, and the cartoon possibility of a fly getting drunk is enough to bring a snort out of me, and the kind of levity I need right now. It's funny how something so incidental can be the thing which breaks a downward spiral. I consider the idea of getting tanked with my new buddy here in cyberspace and it's got me laughing hard now. *Fuck … I must be more on the edge than I thought.* Maybe I should ask it if it knows where Treece is and expect some kind of high-pitched voice roll out the answer. My laughter is more like mania, and probably is.

A sudden blackout plunges everything into darkness and I get up and walk to the window, and watch this quadrant power down block by block. Vehicle lights keep a level of illumination, and street vendors switch to whatever means they have to stay trading through the outage. The skyline is void of its normally constant photo-neon and the only thing I can see periodically casting its light over the urban sprawl is the VTI logo from the French quarter.

The cynic in me thinks this is subliminal advertising—'program your captive audience inside your programme.' Couple that with the addictive qualities of CTs and it'll keep them coming back for more. Maybe that's true, or maybe it's just something else entirely, like Baptiste & Co putting as much realism into all of this as possible. I've no idea and I guess I'll never know.

Whatever the case, it's proved a healthy distraction and I'm ready to get back to finding my mark. I transfer the safe house data Spader coughed up to the Grav and get my things together. There's still firelight on the broadway below, with accident investigators running procedure on Maddox's carrier wreckage. It pulled a sizeable crowd, which hasn't thinned yet and I think it best I disappear before I get held up by anyone wanting answers.

The tenants in my building know exactly who I am and what I do, and for the most part, tend not to get involved in any of my business. But this escapade is a little different, because I don't normally blow up the block on any given Sunday. It's strange taking off from the pad without the usual bank of neon boilerplate in my field of view, and I'm a little disorientated on the jump into traffic.

The grid reference puts the syndicate bolthole square in the docklands. Makes sense, as a great deal of their trafficking activities will doubtless pass through there. I'm going to get port officials up my ass so dodging their checkpoints seems the best way to go. I know a spot where the automated sentry cover is blind and about half a klick from there is a sewer system substation. It's unmanned, and I've used it before to get access to other port locations.

It means putting my ride on the ground but I have a couple of pieces of tech on board which will keep it safe and undetected. Getting out, I arm the bolt-thrower cell which will discharge a nasty kick of electricity to any would-be thieves, and then engage the black market software Zheng recently supplied, to stand and watch the whole thing cloak in shadow. Sitting as it is in a recess beneath suspended rail freight, it's completely hidden by its cover of darkness.

Satisfied, I keep to the shadows myself and head towards the substation. It's calm after the earlier downpour but the general damp air of the docks pervades. What's washed by light glistens on a backdrop of black and grey, chiselled from a stark set of rigid lines. It's all concrete, steel, and sectional fencing here, with everything functional and designed to keep grabbing hands off valuable cargo.

Vast sentinel towers loom over everything and I hear the odd hum of a drone pass over. I've learnt the art of dodging their detection and it's only mere minutes before I'm at the bottom of an access ladder, and running a bypass on the door lock. Docklands security is one of the best in the business because it has to be, but there's nothing which can't be overcome by having the right black market tech. Everything that gets invented usually has an available solution within a matter of days, undoubtedly due to some insider selling the information to the highest bidder.

It's an easy break-in, even with access codes changing on rotation as they do. Inside, the low-level floor lighting runs the length of a single corridor to a T-junction. I've got a holo-page up and it's keeping me on track with co-ordinates, but I might have to deal with a manual lock at the far end if it emerges to a grille of sorts. Nothing I haven't tackled before. I hear a distant something. It's reverberating in here and the volume's increasing with every step I take.

There's what sounds like jeering, en masse, punctuated by the sound of growling dogs. A fight I'm guessing, with those in attendance laying bets on the blood sport. Sure enough, as I round the last corner to an overhead grille, I peer through at the large gathering in what appears to be a sizeable warehouse. The noise is almost thunderous now, but I can hear the clash of the combatants at the heart of it. It's funny how I was thinking about dogs earlier.

There's a lot of money in this game. Big names in the criminal elite have prize-fighters of their own. I recall a tale from years ago where the rivalry between two bosses got so out of control that one of them took to chainsawing the other's pit bull, and had it delivered back to him piece by piece. In terms of a message it's pretty powerful, and no different in concept to two animals tearing each other to shreds in the ring.

They'll always hit each other where it hurts. As for this fight, I'm going to have to wait until it's over and get topside when its spectators have dispersed. I'm in no danger of being discovered; too much happening up there. Time to sit back, spark a cigar, and consider all the angles before I march headlong into a potential Soul Syndicate shitstorm on the other side of that grille.

Head-on Collision

It's pretty obvious what Vargas told me is total bullshit. *So what's his real agenda? Why have me chase a ghost down a rabbit hole?* I need to focus and try to figure this out because I might just come unstuck if I don't. The fight's raging on above me and it's a little hard to think. One thing that's bugging me is seeing that Aeroquad outside my safe zone. Whoever it was saw me for sure and got the hell out of there in a hurry. I'm almost positive he had the look of one of JT's crew, but I can't be sure.

It's got me a little rattled, as it's the one thing which keeps gnawing away at me. So why would Vargas put me in this shitshow, assuming Treece is just a cover story? What would be the purpose of taking me out of circulation for two days? The only thing I can think of is that he needed me to be off the scene for some reason, but there's nothing I can put my finger on.

No matter what the answer is I'm stuck in this now and something tells me if I find Treece, I might just find out the truth. Beyond that grille is what I'm guessing is a small army of Soul Syndicate stooges and very possibly the man I'm looking for. I've got plenty of tricks up my sleeve but I doubt I can tackle all of them in one assault without using grenades, and that would be a bad idea for a handful of reasons.

The only plan that makes sense is to sit tight and wait for the fight to play out, before I make a move. I'm guessing there will be at least one high-level representative out there, someone with a stake in the outcome. I'd probably be able to zero him on sight, but knowing these fuckers, it probably wouldn't hand me any leverage in the hunt for my mark. They'd watch a boss die in a heartbeat knowing it would open up an opportunity to rise. So I'm going to have to come at this sideways if I'm gonna come out on top.

I figure when it's done there's still going to be a handful of foot soldiers on site. The masses will disperse but logic dictates there has to be assets here which need a round-the-clock security detail. If they keep moving Treece, like I've been told, then I'm going to need an intercept advantage, as I can't keep chasing a ghost from one point to the next. Someone has to know a current location for him if he's not here, or at least a transit schedule. That's what these guys do—move bodies, so their operation is slick and designed to keep any would-be hounds off the scent. Thinking of which, the battle beyond the grille seems to be reaching its climax, judging by the spike in spectator volume. Undoubtedly it won't be too much longer before another defeated dog gets tossed into a dumpster outside and ends up being a rats' banquet.

A further twenty minutes or so sees the warehouse pretty much cleared, with the distant sounds of conversation diminishing. The grille's lock springs easy, and I keep to the shadows on the way to the crap-house on the bay side of the interior. I scoped a grunt heading that way, and it's the perfect opportunity to get some answers without having to tackle a group of them, and for things to get noisy.

With the amount of time he's been in there so far, I assume he's seated in a cubicle which will afford the cover I need to gain the advantage. Light pours out of the back office window, and I can see three or four more goons inside. Their loud exchanges drift across the open space -

one freshly stained with combatants' blood. They seem engrossed in what they're doing, so 'Joe Solo' should be an easy takedown. At the crap-house door I hear whistling beyond which totally confirms my hunch.

Unholstering my piece, purely to use its knuckleduster guard, I lean against the door and open it a crack. There's a flickering light inside and a pretty heady stink that's wanting out. God, I move in such high-class circles. Six bays stand against the outer wall and only one has its door closed—the same that has the 'wondrous' sounds of mid-flow gases coming from it. I keep forgetting this is all virtual, as the realism even extends to shit particles. There's just that certain thing about someone else's 'output' that makes you want to gag and it's taking all my focus not to. I binge a little on the good air outside the room, then duck in.

Given the corrupted atmosphere inside, it isn't difficult to hold my breath as I walk gingerly towards the cubicle. I suddenly haul up as the idea I should've used my urban-lite respirator before making an entrance hits home. *Idiot.* I unclip it from my belt and the auto-fastener does its thing. *Thank fuck. I was beginning to really hate this idea.* Breathing shit-free air, I walk on.

There's quite a performance coming out of cubicle four, and I'm guessing that the spatter pattern from his nose, which is imminent, isn't too far removed from a wholly different one on the other side of that door. Clicking the safety on my piece, so that it doesn't accidentally discharge when I hit him, I'm now standing about two feet away from the sliver of a door that separates us. I have a quandary to ponder. *Do I let him finish, or do I slap him around while he's 'dropping the kids off at the pool'?*

Rationale kicks in, and tells me it's probably wise to let him get to empty, because though virtual, I'd still just as not have my footwear standing in any of it. It seems an age before the flush, but when it comes it's a whistling, absent-minded foot soldier who walks onto my duster. He's done quite a bit of 'dropping', only this time it's him that's heading south … onto his knees to be exact, totally winded. I put a second strike to his gut via my boot this time just to hammer home the message and then drag his ass out of there. Now, propped up against the opposite wall he's struggling but still with it, as I remove the safety from my firearm and press the business end into his right eye socket.

"We're gonna play a game of lies and lost chances. I'm going to ask you things. You're going to lie to me, and so you're going to piss away the opportunity to take a dump tomorrow. It's a pretty simple game so don't bother asking me what the rules are. I'm sure you'll pick it up as we go along, with you being the fucking genius you are. Is this all making sense?"

He gives what I take as an understanding of all that and so I get the ball rolling.

"How many Syndicate stooges are in that backroom?"

Five fingers get displayed.

"Including you?"

The head dips slowly in what's an awkward nod.

"Where's Treece?"

He sniggers … in a way I'm taking to mean 'fuck you.'

A loaded Magnum-Drive weighs roughly six and a half pounds. Couple that with a guy weighing 220lbs suddenly shifting his weight against it, and you've got a pretty awesome-looking black eye waiting to flower. He squirms as the pressure's applied and I stifle his reflex response with my free hand.

"There's four other cockroaches back there I can question, so it's not like you're holding all the aces in the pack here. We can always change the game to the one where

I grab that soap dispenser there and use it to muffle the muzzle discharge from this gun. Your head will come off, but at least the cleaning fluid will go some way to tackling the mess in here."

He grunts through my fingers in what I take as willingness to cooperate.

"That a boy."

I move the gun to his temple and now the only weight he feels is from the weapon itself.

"Last time, where's Treece?"

"He ain't here. I mean, not in this place. He's sitting tight on the docks, sure."

I take a second to figure something.

"And there'll be a password, right? That only a few will know."

He grins, which tells me this sack of shit ain't in the loop on that one.

I grin back.

It's just a second between grabbing the soap dispenser and the moment his head opens up all over the wall.

Fuck … I was wrong. The cleaning fluid ain't done a thing about the mess.

***

The goon cluster in the back office is engrossed in a poker game and doesn't read my approach.

"That would be a real bad move," I say to the one who looks up and goes for his piece under the table.

The rest freeze. One has his back to me and those left and right slowly turn to take in the sight of this intruder. My urban-lite has been stowed but I'm betting my hat has my face in shadow anyways. I stay in the doorway, but keep my gun aimed squarely at the bald head of the guy facing me.

"You're all gonna show your hands, and by that I don't mean the cards."

There's uncertainty, quick glances exchanged, before they slowly comply by putting hands palm down on the table.

"Now I hate to use clichés but the stakes just went up, gentlemen. Oh, and if you're thinking your fifth man is gonna ghost me when we're in the middle of this peachy little convo, you'll find that possibility went down the crapper two minutes ago."

A stiff silence hangs heavy. They're itching to go for their guns and it'll just take one to shift an inch to set the others off. I can't afford for that to happen, not until I've bagged the intel I'm after.

"Not the first tight spot you've been in, granted. But before any of you gets to thinking 'we'll get bloody but we'll take him down', it's only right and proper you know who you're dealing with. Reverend's the name … and I've been in the burial business since the war got done with me. You'd best keep my mood all light and whimsy, else this here heater will be turning four syndicate boys into a jigsaw puzzle."

The change in body language tells me they know the name, but is it enough to keep any dumb bravado in check?

"Sure, you like to gamble, but I'm betting not so much with your lives. You. Yeah, you, baldy. I'm gonna give you the choice. It's on you who lives or dies. I'm gonna start with some questions. Each time you lie, I drop a sidekick … comprende?"

His eyes sweep the other three and he gives me a slight, nervous nod. The tension is like invisible concrete.

"So, Treece. I know he's dockside. I also know you syndicate types like to keep your assets in near perpetual motion, but that game ends right here."

I leave the statement hanging to get the point across.

"What's the holding unit number?"

He takes a sharp intake of breath and stares at the tabletop. I can practically hear those cogs going round between his ears. I prime the hammer on my piece and aim it at the scumbag left of him.

"It's unit X-19," says baldy.

The bullet hits square in the neck, separating the head which finds its way into the corner of the room, as the torso covers the trio in a spray of blood. They're stunned, and are torn between wiping their faces and obeying my command to keep their hands on the table. It slowly drips off them, giving baldy enough time to consider dishing up more lies. He looks up at me and meets my gaze.

"Unit V-21 … V-21," he says, with a nod.

Scumbag on the right displays a subtle frown, enough for me to grasp its meaning. The second bullet blows out the spine, lungs and rib cage of the creep sat opposite baldy, and no doubt it screams past his ear before being buried in the wall behind. He gets covered in kill number two, the remains of which are sliding out of the chair as the tabletop is now nothing but red.

"It's impossible to have a Dead Man's Hand show up twice in a poker game, but I'm just full of tricks, baldy."

Sitting there, covered in gore, I think he's finally getting the message.

"Yeah, it's erm … it's G-14."

"And the password?"

It takes a few seconds more, but he spills the intel.

"River-Mai."

There are moments when everything seems to bleach away into the dark days of living. Here I am, for all intents and purposes asleep, acting out some deranged fantasy inside the artificial guts of a supercomputer, and my very soul is being fucked with. My dead daughter's name … are you fucking kidding me? There's just the smallest trace of a grin on that fat, bald head of his. My mind's on fire but I'm momentarily paralysed. I'm supposed to process this and keep a level head? My reflexes do the things my brain can't conceive, with a finger connecting with the rapid fire switch on the Magnum-Drive and the trigger feeling the iron grip of another.

It seems slow motion, as I feel the gun's constant recoil and the scene becomes an explosion of wood, flesh and tumbling pieces. Everything in the arc of rage comes apart in the same turbulent way my broken life's been lived. This carnage. These total motherfuckers. That's all the Narcoplex I need right here. Before I know it, the gun's jammed open, with a full clip spent in a crescendo of casing chimes around me. The air's thick with the smell of grapheno-cordite and that jigsaw puzzle I talked about earlier is laid out across half the room. There's just an eerie stillness now and the gun's getting lowered kinda staggered as I'm not really in control of what's happening.

Push a finger into my still raw 'family wound' and I'm gonna be tearing down the world every goddamn time.

I don't recall leaving the building, but here I am smoking a No-Glo and drifting through the docks on autopilot. The bay is busy with traffic and the lights are bokeh orbs on the water. There's a breeze up, carrying the scent of boat engines and a city bleeding its waste into the shimmering expanse. Despite my mindset, it would seem I had the presence of mind to think ahead. I'm carrying the head of poker player one, which I've stuck onto a pry bar that was sitting atop a packing crate. It's dark, and who knows, I might just get lucky with what I have planned.

Sector G is about a hundred yards ahead. Judging by the numerics on the rows next to me, fourteen will be near the waterfront, as the high numbers are right where I'm walking. It's about a mile at a guess, which is just fine as it gives me time to get my head back in the game. Right now, I'm a ball of fury, and it won't serve me well when taking out the protection Treece will have around him. I need my wits about me and this haul across the docks will get that back. Security drones buzz in the distance, reminding me I need to stay sharp.

When this is done there'll be hell to pay. Once I'm out of Baptiste's cyber circus, Vargas better arm himself to the teeth. I'll take whatever a mission throws my way, but when I'm fucked with from the start, mine shall be a righteous vengeance. I've been played all down the line on this but ignored that inner voice which told me at the start this was a bad idea. Crime lord or no, he's just a man, and I've buried more than I care to remember. After a half hour the storage unit looms, beckoning to bring an end to this charade.

***

I hold the head in position. There's an inspection hatch in the door. Crouching down, I knock and wait, hoping the guard doesn't shine a torch on the 'visitor.' Seconds pass before I hear footfalls beyond followed by a slide of the panel.

"Erm yeah, that you, Wes?"

"Yep. River-Mai," I answer, gruffly.

As quick as it opened, the hatch closes and I hear the deadbolt clear its housing on the other side. Standing, I throw my shoulder against the door and the momentum carries me through whilst throwing the first guard against the wall. A second rises from a chair in the room and gets the Wes head on a pry bar slammed into his temple. As he goes down, I drop the grim artifact and pull a throwing knife from my sleeve sheath. Loosed, it thuds into the chest of the first gorilla, who goes down mid step to collide with his already dazed partner, sending him sprawling. He makes a half roll to attempt getting up but my boot slams onto his throat to pin him. The chair's scatter cushion makes a handy impromptu silencer, as I bury my gun's muzzle into it and feed him high-speed metalwork.

It's over in seconds and my mark is doubtless beyond that inner door. I retrieve my knife and listen. Muffled sounds rise and fall in the next room. I can't discern what's making them but I don't get a sense there's any extra on-site security. Still, keeping gun in hand, I work the handle on the final barrier between me and my mark. The audio climbs as the door swings open and the room is a palette of changing light. Its source is a large wall-mounted screen playing host to vintage cinema. When I say vintage, I'm talking early decades twentieth century … stuff from the vaults that doesn't see the light of day anymore.

The Wizard of Oz is playing out on screen, the scene where Dorothy and the scarecrow are skipping along the yellow brick road. The man on the sofa, who can only be Treece, is engrossed. A book sits open on the low table in front of him, as does a bottle and two glasses which are flanked by an old-style cigarette burning slowly down on the edge of an ashtray. He laughs a little as the scarecrow stumbles, before turning to me and greeting me with a broad smile.

"Please, take a seat. Join me, Mr. Hendrix. I'll pour you a drink and we can get acquainted."

He gestures to the sofa amid fixing our drinks. He's open and genuine, and matches Treece's mugshot to a T. Done, he offers me the drink and picks the cigarette up for a drag. I'm completely thrown. *What the fuck is this? Could this shit get any more sideways?*

"How the fuck do you know who I am?"

Arm extended, my drink in hand, he frowns as if it isn't obvious.

"Well, if you'd just join me, I shall explain."

He lifts the glass a little higher to entice and smiles warmly as I relent.

"That's the spirit, Mr. Hendrix. There's no need for caution here. You must be a little weary at this point. Some rest and your favourite rum can only help."

Keeping my piece handy, I go ahead and take the glass from him, and set an ass cheek on the arm of the sofa. He chugs on the cigarette again before raising his glass in a toast.

"To a successful mission."

My jaw must be somewhere near the floor. I've obviously missed about a thousand things in all of this. The drink's aroma tells me it's Pacific Port and I'm torn between smashing the glass in his face and thinking 'fuck it, knock it back, have another, hell, drain the whole bottle.' A slug goes down. That familiar taste. The emptied glass, as it's lowered, is like a fisheye lens which ensnares the words on the page of the book, before the downward motion sweeps it across the number centred at the bottom. It's a brief distortion, but enough to magnify the numeric, which hits home like a ton of bricks. The hardback is open at page 57, and my understanding of everything is in freefall.

Glass set on the table, I use the gun barrel to flip the front cover over to see the book title. Yep, there it is, right there: *The Master Key: An Electrical Fairy Tale* by L. Frank Baum. Treece takes a drink but eyes me in the process, looking for a reaction I'm guessing. If I wasn't so numb there'd be one. Honestly, I've got nothing left. It's like the wind has been taken out of my sails and every limb feels heavy. I'm on the verge of just shooting Treece and waiting out the rest of my time in immersion. Killing Vargas, out in the real world, is all I care about now.

"I'd assumed you'd have a whole line of questions for me, but it seems not," says Treece.

I exhale slow and hard. "You're a decoy, right?"

He looks at the floor, and that's all I need to confirm that thought.

"I guess you could say I'm the wizard behind the curtain, and like old Oz there, not a very good one," he says.

My mind's racing. Equal parts anger and bewilderment.

"But unlike Dorothy, I'm afraid you don't get to click your heels together and go home, Mr. Hendrix," he adds.

Now he's got my full attention.

"The fuck you say?"

Red rag to a bull. I'm having that answered no matter what.

"Well, those with eyes on the situation know exactly where you are in this construct. X marks the spot as they say, so I believe it's probably mere minutes before they pull the plug on you and it's game over."

He takes another drag on his cigarette and blows the smoke my way, the gesture followed by a thin smile.

If I ever had a grand 'oh fuck' moment, this is it. Everything zeros into focus. This whole technicolour mindfuck was simply a way to get me vulnerable and dusted. When the wires are ripped out on the other side I'm brain-drained in Vargas' perfectly executed manoeuvre. Treece takes in my epiphany and the thin smile turns to a sinister grin. There's even a jackal-like hiss of laughter and the look I get is one of 'oh, the boy just upped and realised'. *Do I kill him? Does it even matter? I'm screwed regardless …*

I just roar my rage. *How the fuck could I have been so blind?* Never ignore your gut. This artificial room is the corner I've painted myself into. Back on my feet, I'm pacing back and forth, thinking, seething, cursing. It helps a little when I aim my gun at a sneering Treece, but only for a split second as the crushing realisation his death won't stop a thing comes crashing back down on me. I'm frantic. Less scared to die than being outdone by a rat like Vargas. The only sense in this is Baptiste must have been complicit. I could be unplugged at any …

It's a slow-motion fall with the grinning decoy in my failing vision. The phantom clock I'd had to concentrate on to access now dances before my eyes, with its countdown in hyper-acceleration. Everything begins to disintegrate. Dropping to my knees, the gun goes sprawling and the light is getting pushed quickly to the centre of the scene by a black vice which is pressing in from either side. What I am is being crushed out of existence in a pixelating collapse. There's a building pressure, a waning reality, in the moment before the outside force pile-drives the inner resistance. And then it buckles to compress to a single point of light, which flatlines.

***

I'm grasping something solid. Something which provides a true resistance. Eyes splice open with everything flickering around me as I arc in restraints and grip the arms of the chair. Baptiste. Miss Argyle in his grasp. A lab technician. There's my thrashing, a pain so intense I think it's going to fracture my skull, and the sense of a needle point at my arm. A super rush and a fading. All goes dark once again.

***

"Mr. Hendrix. Mr. Hendrix."

My name punctuated by clicking fingers.

"Mr. Hendrix, are you with us?"

Half-light, blurred images. An overpowering sense of ache.

"He's coming round. Elevate the back support," says another voice.

I get a sense I'm sitting up now.

"Mr. Hendrix, I'm just going to give you another injection. This will help you stabilise," says a technician.

I don't even feel the metalwork go in but he's in focus now. Nausea's a bitch.

"You're very lucky, Mr. Hendrix. Had I been mere seconds late, then I'm afraid Miss Argyle would have removed the second neuro-coupling and we wouldn't be having this conversation," Baptiste says.

Argyle? What's she got to do with this … whatever this is?

"What you just said means absolutely nothing to me," I reply.

"I'm not surprised at all. You could've quite easily died, Mr. Hendrix. I suggest you get some rest and we can talk later. Our technicians will be on hand to get you through this difficult transition."

"I will of course monitor your progress but you will have to be our guest for longer than was anticipated," Baptiste adds.

Whatever cocktail was in that syringe is warming me nicely and Baptiste goes out of focus once more.

Day Four, After Forced VR Extraction

"How are you feeling, Mr. Hendrix?"

Baptiste's question hangs for a spell as I look out across the city from his office at V-Trance. Without turning, I answer.

"A little like my old self again. We've not discussed what went on that day. Care to enlighten me now that I'm packed for the walk to the gate?"

He leans back in his chair and tilts his head a tad.

"Well it's really quite simple. Miss Argyle, whilst in my employ, just so happened to be in the employ of Mr. Vargas too. I became suspicious of her motives after a security audit discovered her site visit during a time of supposed absence."

He steeples his fingers, then continues.

"It's clear she used that particular day to set up the necessary protocols to deal with your demise. These things were meant to facilitate that, but also help cover her tracks in the wake of your passing. Had I not been wise to her movements, she would have succeeded, and Mr. Vargas would be celebrating your extraction from NeuTokyo's darker market activities I believe."

Again, without turning, I answer.

"So you're my hero? I have to live with 'that'? I guess my life just took a real sharp downturn," I quip.

He grins, and has an equally dry comeback.

"Just like we here at V-Trance Industries don't get to choose our customers, Mr. Hendrix."

I laugh, in what seems the first time in an age. It's funny, a guy I had zero respect for, in a profession which seemed outlandish to me, turns out to be one who hands this broken soldier some hope in humanity.

"Speaking of which, what do I owe you for the extended stay?"

He gets up, walks over to me and offers his hand.

"Nothing, Mr. Hendrix. Think of it as an investment on my part."

I eye him suspiciously, at which he simply raises an eyebrow and smiles knowingly. Clasping his hand, I'm left wondering what's simmering beneath the surface of that exchange.

"What's your next move?" he asks.

I turn and look back out across the city. Somewhere out there Vargas is undoubtedly prepared for my arrival.

"Oh, let's just say I have a dinner date for the last supper."

He frowns, eyes me keenly and then pats me on the shoulder.

"Just deserts, I'm thinking," he says, with a wink.

The Stuff of Urban Legend

One of the more recent stories added to the Vargas canon tells of a gathering gone wrong. Associates, including those of the city's notorious biker gang, had come together in their common interest in the disposal of a problematic bounty hunter. If the rumours are to be believed, all were slain, having been decapitated midway through dessert. The bodies were still sat at the table the morning after, discovered by the cleaning crew which had been hired to mop up after the event. It is noted the clean-up operation apparently ran to taking full advantage of the crime lord's demise, in the emptying of the on-site safe—a thing requiring a Vargas retinal scan. In a city where the rats are always looking to eat their own, and climb to the top of the pile, this tale is as believable as any other. They say if you can find The Reverend, he could give you chapter and verse on this, but that's a story for another day.

A Pledge of Allegiance

In his bid for office on the Presidential campaign trail, Senator Kip Wheeler promised America's sons and daughters [its shattered souls of war] would be compensated way beyond 'the demeaning and limited way they'd so far been treated under countless administrations beforehand.'

Should he, by the will of the nation, be chosen to represent the hopes and desires of everyday Americans, then he'd ensure that those who'd made so many sacrifices would be repaid unequivocally, with the introduction of revolutionary life-affirming support programmes.

That was thirty-seven months ago …

The Outer Lands Military Compound - 2102

It was a bleak Tuesday morning when the colonel's tiltrotor carrier touched down on the helipad. The warbird's all-electric drive barely made a sound as it delivered him for the site's second annual inspection. An Atlantic storm cell had brought bad weather to the island for days and it showed no sign of letting up anytime soon. Handing his raincoat to facilities staff, he received a hot cup of coffee in exchange, which he acknowledged with a nod of approval. Flanked by a lesser ranking officer and the compound's operational commander, he walked through sectors C and D before finally entering the doctor's office at the end of the corridor. A Newton's Cradle clicked away on the desktop and the room's occupant was engrossed in the data displayed on a holographic monitor, so much so, he failed to register the arrival of the three military figures in the room.

A moment of dismay was shared by the men in uniform, before the colonel cleared his throat and made his slight irritation known.

"It's always good to see a man so entrenched in his duties, but if you don't mind my dear doctor, I've spent nearly two hours airborne and the better part of that riding through a hail of piss and fury. It'd be darn civilised of you to at least acknowledge my existence."

"Oh, forgive me gentlemen … I was … distracted shall we say," said the man in the white coat rising from his chair, first offering his hand to the colonel, and then to his accompanying lieutenant.

"Please, be seated, and may I offer the lieutenant here a hot drink too?"

Lieutenant Cross smiled an acknowledgement, but one short-lived at the colonel's response.

"He'll do just fine as is."

The facility's commander, Major Blackmore, took his leave and the three remaining got down to the business at hand, with Cross taking the minutes of the meeting.

"So doctor, where are we another twelve months down the line? What can you tell me about the advancements you've made in your therapeutic modelling?" the colonel inquired.

Reaching out to stop the Newton's Cradle, the head of research and development took a little time to gather his thoughts before answering.

"Since your first inspection, there have been significant advancements in the way we implement the programme. I will explain a few of those right now but I think it best I leave the rest for the subsequent site tour. Are you happy with that?"

The colonel nodded and took another sip of his coffee.

"No doubt you've absorbed everything in our quarterly reports, but I imagine they can be a source of more questions than answers at times," the doctor added.

"We get the main thrust of the data, but some of the detail gets away from our analysts now and then," the lieutenant explained.

"Quite so, and that's to be expected given the fact we're in uncharted territory here. Believe me, there are times when even the best minds on site are left reaching for a satisfactory explanation of what we're presented with on a daily basis."

The doctor paused, glanced at the monitor to jog his memory, and then continued.

"We'd always planned for the long-term effects of such a lengthy operation, and so a great many of the predicted outcomes have indeed come to light. There are, however, a number of findings which have been of particular interest that we hadn't anticipated. Environmental factors have proven to have a latent effect on the experiences of those in our care, and we've also seen evidence of what we deem 'crossover' in character profiling. I shall explain both. We are finding the physical space we provide each patient is playing a subliminal role in shaping their subconscious models. I'll provide you with some actual references on the site tour, and a detailed analysis will be included in my supporting submissions. In terms of crossover, it seems historic references are finding their way into the building blocks of any assembled perception."

The colonel rubbed his jaw, leaned back in his chair, and cast a quick sideways glance at the lieutenant. All of that was about as clear as horse shit but he deflected his lack of understanding by addressing Cross.

"You got that down word for word, right?"

"Affirmative," he replied.

The doctor could see the moment was a slightly awkward one, and decided to speed the process along by introducing the site tour somewhat early.

"Perhaps it's best if we conduct the rest of our meeting on foot. I can explain as we go, and I'm sure having various visual references for the things we discuss will help your understanding of the processes involved."

The colonel nodded and gestured that the doctor proceed. He led them back the way they had come and entered sector D. A one hundred-metre squared space housed all manner of equipment. Life support systems, monitoring consoles, dedicated aisle generators, and row upon row of stasis pods suspended from the structure's metal roof beams.

"As you can see, each subject is in deep trance, but I will refer to what I said earlier," said the doctor.

"When I mentioned environmental factors, what I meant was the environment of the pods themselves. Suspended as they are in the inter-spacial fluid, our subjects are experiencing direct contact with the suspension mass. In other words, when we periodically bring our subjects out of deep state, time and again we have accounts of a sense of a moist atmosphere being present in their individual constructs. That may just be how the weather is perceived within that virtual arena, for example, or even as a damp facet of buildings and other enclosed spaces. It's fascinating to think these subconscious perceptions are forming crossover experiences, along with historic references."

Cross looked up from his note taking, and prompted the doctor.

"Can you explain 'historic references'?"

Happy to have that clarified, the colonel listened intently.

"Of course. Quite simply, our subjects have experienced a great deal in their lives before being immersed in this programme. It's inevitable that some fragments of their former existence will be brought into play within whatever scenarios they perceive in their new realities," the doctor explained.

Cross admitted slight confusion, in that his understanding was subjects would be unaware of their former lives whilst in deep state suspension. The doctor brought him up to speed by explaining that past and current experiences were a carefully interwoven perception for the immersed. This allowed for a smooth transition and therefore acceptance in the individual. Something a jarring change would have jeopardised. Each participant was extensively assessed and interviewed prior to their immersion, with their new reality being fundamentally based on what they'd asked for.

For the first time, this made sense to both soldiers.

"So, after what you've just said, are there any instances of where there has been adverse reactions to the programme's purpose?" asked the colonel.

Careful not to allow any negative reporting have any potentially damning consequences for the future of project, the doctor answered with caution.

"There have been some issues, but that is to be expected given we are dealing with intelligent cargo, gentlemen. The human mind is a powerful tool and not easily shoe-horned into alien scenarios which might give rise to a sense of self-preservation. Like all things in this, we manage these outcomes, as modelling and conjecture can only give us so much mileage. There comes a point where direct experience is the only way we can gather the intel and adjust our methods accordingly."

"And what of the medications involved, any anomalies there?" the colonel pressed.

"Well, Narcoplectin Nitrate, which we use to induce and maintain a deep stasis, was an extensively trialled drug way in advance of this project. To date we've seen no adverse reactions nor tolerance issues in any of the subjects. I don't foresee any change in that but we will of course monitor usage in line with protocol."

Seemingly satisfied with the doctor's practical approach, the colonel pursued another line of questioning.

"When can we say this whole shooting match is a runaway success?"

The doctor laughed a little, before calling for caution.

"We're not quite there yet, gentlemen. However, I don't foresee it taking too much longer before we have all the trial data available and projected annual budgetary requirements going forward."

The colonel nodded his approval. They stopped momentarily by a pod. A male former soldier occupied the unit. Equipped with just an integrated respirator and virtual reality headset, the ex-marine was damaged goods like all others in suspension. The colonel's gaze settled on the pod display.

"Well I'll be …" he remarked.

The unit on the panel read: Hendrix, Balaam - I/Ex Date: 9/23/2101. He stood and pondered for a second.

"I knew Hendrix was in the programme. Of course I did, but what are the chances of coming across him amid all these veterans? This guy was a helluva marine. And, believe it or not, doctor, saved my life back in the war."

He stared in admiration before continuing.

"We were in the kill zone. It wasn't going our way. We'd been ordered out but were pinned down. This soldier walked through fire to haul my ass outta there. I owe him my life."

Lost in thought, he put a hand on the pod's glass hood and tapped it lightly.

"What we're doing for these soldiers is the very least we can do," he added.

Staring at the broken form inside, he seemed to relive the damage Hendrix had endured. The left arm was completely gone, and the left leg off at the knee. The whole left side, up the neck and onto the face was a map of scar tissue, where surgeons had put the man back together.

"What's his story?" the colonel asked.

The doctor thought for a moment.

"If I recall correctly, this candidate opted to pick up his life exactly where it had suffered catastrophic ruin. Most opt for a setting which is far removed from a place of conflict, but in his case, he wished to carry on at ground zero so-to-speak."

He paused a second, to recall more information, then carried on.

"It's interesting because he asked it be set in China. Well, the newly acquired territory anyways. When Tokyo fell, and his life fell apart in the final battle, I think he felt his new life should begin where the old one ended. In terms of continuity it makes sense. He wanted to be a bounty hunter. He wanted family too. The main elements were coded and then his mind would do the rest. In the early trials he'd emerge from immersion and write down fragments here and there which our technicians would mull over in order to try and make sense of his virtual experience. One time he wrote this."

He gestured to Cross for his holo-notepad and pen, which the lieutenant gave up. The doctor hastily scribbled something and showed them. It read: SET IT CH · IN · A.

"At first it seemed just as he'd requested. His mind reaffirming we set his new existence in China, albeit penning it with the word 'in' integral to the word 'China'. But on subsequent extractions from immersion he'd penned something different."

He scribbled again and showed them the altered version. It read: SIN:THETICA.

"As you can imagine, we simply thought this was the product of a confused mind. One struggling with what was real and what was intended. It was only when one of our young technicians, Jackson, pointed out it was an anagram of the original instruction, did we begin to see those elements of crossover I spoke of earlier."

He handed the pad and pen back to Cross, who looked just as confused as the colonel.

"It's an example of where a subject has taken elements of conversations or thought processes and reassembled them as something else on the other side," the doctor explained.

Now it made sense but fuelled a question from Cross.

"So what does SIN:THETICA mean to Hendrix?" he asked.

The doctor shrugged.

"Very difficult to say, lieutenant. It seems to change at every extraction, but it's definitely a recurring theme. I often wonder if it's a loop which is snaring the mind, but I really can't say for sure."

There was a long silence.

"Well, I think we've covered the main grey areas, unless you have any further questions for me, gentlemen?"

The colonel snapped from his thought process.

"You're quite right, doctor. Cross and I will continue to conduct our site tour to record visuals for the top brass. If there's work you need to get back to, by all means."

"I'll have nurse Argyle accompany you for the rest of the inspection. She's very knowledgeable and should be able to answer any further questions that may arise. Oh, and please, before your departure, do make use of our canteen facilities. I recommend the steak. Done to perfection it's the best I've come across."

"Thank you, Baptiste. It goes without saying the Corps appreciates all you're doing for these war-torn veterans," said the colonel, shaking his hand.

The diner was an interesting experience. The scientific brigade weren't the only oddball characters to be found at the facility. A cleaner, named Kravitz, did his level best to get under the feet of the visiting uniforms, mopping literally over the colonel's well-polished footwear, whilst asking a thousand and one inappropriate questions regarding his visit. Cross made a note to have his employment situation assessed back at base. The aforementioned technician, Jackson, provided the soldiers with a little more insight into the workings of the programme, before asking the colonel what his recreational drug of choice happened to be and pledging a slick and unhindered supply if needed. Needless to say, it did not go down well at all.

But perhaps the most interesting and quirky duo on site were the canteen manager and her avian sidekick. Ma Tsingtao and her Macaw, Cyrus, provided a little light entertainment during the visit. Her with her flirtatious ways and the bird with its mimicry of many of the facility's staff. Back outside, with the storm abated, Cross boarded the tiltrotor first, leaving his superior to take a last lingering look at the complex. Lost in thought, it took a good minute before Colonel James Templeton Danzig stepped aboard the warbird and signed off the visit with a salute to all those who'd given their old lives for their country.

Just So You Know ...
Everything

In a standard issue ammo box, inside a locker in the Outer Lands Military Compound, a collection of mementos were hidden from the light of day. Among prized possessions of a former life, a book lay closed with a dog-eared marker placed at a certain page. It was a hardback, with a worn dust jacket, titled *The Master Key: An Electrical Fairy Tale* by L. Frank Baum.

Inside, an inscription on the half title page read as follows:

Merry Christmas, Balaam!

This book belonged to my great, great grandfather and so I thought the time was right to pass it on down to you.

Just like the main character in this story, I hope one day you'll be able to have a fantastical adventure of your own, fuelled by your incredible imagination!

Lots of love

Mom

XX

ACKNOWLEDGEMENTS

Heather and Steve (BGP), my community people on socials, friends, and family. Steve specifically for the edits, Steph for the formatting, and Alex for the cover. Oh, and this fine English crumpet topped with melted Cheddar cheese that's going down rather well with a mug of tea as I write this.

About the Author

Keith Anthony Baird has written a number of works, all of which can be found using your browser - get busy!

He lives in Cumbria, in the United Kingdom, on the edge of the Lake District National Park.

Twitter/X -https://twitter.com/kabauthor

ABOUT THE ARTIST

Alexander Way-B is dyslexic, has a background in art and design, and grew up in the south of England. He has travelled extensively, and lived and worked in Japan, and France. He is both an illustrator and author.

Content Warnings

Violence
Profanity
Drug and alcohol references
PTSD

More From Brigids Gate Press

In the Grimdark Strands of the Spinneret

by Keith Anthony Baird

Betrayal brings grave ending to a noble bloodline. Forced to flee, its sole surviving heir is spared this fate by the timely intervention of a haunter of the wilds. In his charge, the maiden embraces the lore of the dark arts and rises to become the watch-keep of the woods. As decades pass, with her legend growing, the 'witch of root and earth' weaves subtle deceits in a tangled web of vengeance.

But will there be a fairy tale ending, or will poisoned legacies and pacts with dark forces see ambition unravel in her relentless pursuit of power?

Bloody, and brilliantly realised, Baird's dark fantasy nightmare spins a lavish tale of dread, desire, and fantastical fury.

THE FIVE TURNS OF THE WHEEL

BY STEPHANIE ELLIS

Welcome to the Weald. The Five Turns of the Wheel has begun. With each Turn, blood will be spilled, and sacrifices will be made. Pacts will be made … and broken. Will you join the Dance?

In the Weald, the time has come for the Five Turns of the Wheel. Tommy, Betty and Fiddler, the sons of Hweol, Lord of Umbra, have arrived to oversee the sacred rituals … rituals brimming with sacrifice and dripping with blood.

Megan Wheelborn, daughter of Tommy, hatches a desperate plan to free the people of the Weald from the bloody and cruel grip of Umbra, and put an end to its murderous rituals. But success will require sacrifice and blood as well. Will Megan be able to pay the price?

A Man in Winter

by Katie Marie

'A mesmerizing psychological mystery from an author who brings a refreshing new voice to horror. This is a quick read, but one that keeps the reader thoroughly intrigued and entertained from beginning to end.'

—Catherine Cavendish, author of *In Darkness, Shadows Breathe* and *Dark Observation* (coming in September 2022)

Arthur, whose life was devastated by the brutal murder of his wife, must come to terms with his diagnosis of dementia. He moves into a new home at a retirement community, and shortly after, has his life turned upside down again when his wife's ghost visits him and sends him on a quest to find her killer so her spirit can move on. With his family and his doctor concerned that his dementia is advancing, will he be able to solve the murder before his independence is permanently restricted?

A Man in Winter examines the horrors of isolation, dementia, loss, and the ghosts that come back to haunt us.

What Happened at Hawthorne House

by Hadassah Shiradski

In 1926, nine-year-old Rosalyn invents a new game to play with the girls she shares a dormitory with in the Hawthorne House Orphanage. Revolving around a Royal Court, their make-believe game quickly becomes a way to gain some measure of control in their unhappy lives. But when the rules start changing and the stakes start rising, nothing is safe, and Rosalyn finds that she's willing to get her hands dirty in order to be the Queen.

Rosalyn will do *whatever* it takes to wear the crown.

All that's left is to take it.

Visit our website at: www.brigidsgatepress.com